HUNTING THE BEAST

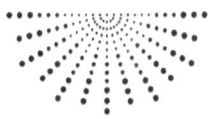

W.T. WATSON

BEYOND THE FRAY
Publishing

ISBN 13: 978-1-954528-02-4

Beyond The Fray Publishing, a division of Beyond The Fray, LLC, San Diego, CA
www.beyondthefraypublishing.com

BEYOND THE FRAY

Publishing

To Stacey, my long-suffering spouse, who sat with me as I blathered about folklore, muttered about plot points, despaired of ever getting my editing 'right' and generally worried over the fate of my created universe. Love and thanks!

To all the many Fortean writers and folklorists who have documented and continue to document the lore of the Phantom Black Dog, werewolves, the Faery and Sasquatch, many thanks to you for hours of creepy reading and the ideas that blossomed into this novel.

CHAPTER ONE

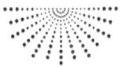

*S*takeouts are not the most interesting part of my jobs but, on this night, the surveillance duty was alright. It was warm for an October night in Buffalo and Chippewa Street was alive with a number of interesting characters. I took a sip of the hot Jamaican Blue I had picked up from the local coffee shop and scanned the street again, trying to parse a werewolf out of the crowd of students and young professionals moving up and down the street.

I'd been told by one of the local witches, a frequent information source, that she had seen a wolf that she did not recognize from the local pack at The Palmero, the local metal bar. Now, it was possible that Alonso Martinez, the Buffalo Pack Alpha, had inducted a new member but, if so, I should have been informed. I am, after all, the Buffalo Region's Black Dog and I am responsible for enforcing the Charter, the laws of the Otherworld, on the werewolf population.

Whether Alonso was holding out on me or we had a rogue wolf in our midst, I needed to know about it so I had been watching the Palermo for several evenings, hoping to encounter the mysterious werewolf.

I had finished my third cup of coffee and was beginning to think that this night was a wash when I spotted the wolf. He had come around the corner from Delaware slowly. He was a young man of average height incongruously wearing aviator shades in the dark night. It was not the silliness of the sunglasses at night that cued me; it was the fact that as soon as he got close to the human crowds people formed an unconscious ring around him.

Humans have worked hard to become rational beings, to ignore the things that go bump in the night, but they have not evolved so far that they do not recognize a predator in their midst. The boy did not even have enough control to damp his inner carnivore so that he could mix with human society. That made him a rogue and my job now was to bring him in.

I exited the car slowly, conscious that sudden movement might alert the werewolf and moved across the street. Even an untrained wolf had uncannily sharp senses so I checked to make certain the wind was blowing in my face before moving closer to my target. I had dressed in black so I blended with the Goth crowd outside the Palermo until I was directly behind my subject. Speaking softly enough that nonhuman ears could not hear me, I murmured, " Listen carefully and do not move. I know what you are. Stand quietly and I promise you that no harm will come to you. Right now, I just want . . . "

I had expected a punch or a kick, even a charging tackle or flat-out flight. I did not anticipate the idiot boy attempting to shift right there in front of me and every human on the block. I felt the sudden inrush of his energy; the leap in his body temperature and the tingling, crawling sensation of his field shifting in preparation for melting his body into another form. He might not have had any training but he had obviously shifted a number of times before. He knew exactly how to do that. I had seconds in which to act before the boy committed a breach of the Charter which would force me to put him down.

Fortunately, I come equipped to handle such nonsense. A

subsonic growl, audible only to the rogue werewolf, escaped me as my magic flared around me. I felt an answering heat rise inside me as I hissed the rune of ice, throwing out my hand to project the spell. The rogue literally froze in place.

Now, if I'd been so inclined, I could have frozen the lad from the inside out, tapped him with my fist and shattered him into a thousand pieces. That's why runes work so well for fighting; they already have an assigned meaning, you can charge them in a second, throw them very quickly and get a predictable result depending on how much energy you pour through them. I had put just enough oomph into the spell to stop all motion but not enough to turn the rogue into an ice cube.

My captive was not so frozen that he could not move his eyes and I realized, as he tried to look past my six plus foot frame that I had company behind me. Normally, I try to move in a way that humans might later recall as very quick but not preternaturally fast. When you have good reason to think that a rogue werewolf's maker might be slipping up behind you though, you dispense with the illusion and just move. I blurred out of the way and turned to face the new threat.

I was through fooling around with these two. In my subsonic voice, audible only to the two wolves, I announced, "Charter Enforcement Officer, I am a Black Dog! You have one chance to cease and desist and come peacefully. Otherwise, I will be forced to take you by whatever measures I deem necessary."

The female werewolf behind me—a very attractive blonde dressed for a night on the town—knew right away that resistance would not end well. My people have a deservedly fierce reputation amongst the werewolves. No wolf with any pack training would willingly oppose a Black Dog.

The female responded instantly by dropping her eyes and holding her hands out where I could see them. The submissive posture eased my tension but the boy had more fight in him. I heard him growl and felt him strain against my magic. I threw a little extra will into the spell and he quieted as I rounded on the female. "Did you make this one?"

The blonde wolf had the good grace not to lie to me. "Yes," she replied simply, "I know I am in violation of the Charter but, please, I beg you for a chance to explain."

I eyed her for a moment, studying her body language and scent for a hint of dissimulation before replying, "I am willing to hear you out but I require your sworn word that you will come in peace."

The female wolf nodded, slowly, intensely aware that she was on very thin ice. "I swear it by all I hold holy."

I looked to the boy. "And this one?"

The blonde moved cautiously up and touched the younger wolf. The shift in her scent and the energy between them told me that the two were more than maker and made. She gave her lover a beseeching look and he muttered a sound that indicated his agreement.

I did not take much stock in the rogue's word but the female wolf seemed to have experience. Oaths taken amongst creatures of my world are binding in ways that humans will never understand. I slowly eased off the will in my spell and the young male collapsed into his lover's waiting arms.

It took the young wolf a couple of minutes to recover from the effects of my spell but, once he was moving again, I walked the two slowly over to The Spot, the coffee joint that I patronized when I was in the area, got them a warm drink and then settled in to listen to their story.

The female was called Nancy Sanderson and she was a lone wolf, made in the Cattaraugus pack shortly after World War II. She had been offered the chance to save her life from leukemia by a friend in the pack but had not taken well to pack life. Once she was trained, the pack allowed her to certify as a lone wolf and she had come to live in Buffalo. She'd been living in the Nickel City ever since and had been working at the University of Buffalo as a research assistant when she met Lon Giffords.

Lon, not knowing that Nancy was literally three times his age, had fallen hard for a young lady who appeared to be a young woman with advanced wildlife tracking skills. The two had worked together in the Adirondacks following up on reports of Eastern Grey Wolves in the area and, though Nancy had resisted his advances in every way she could, eventually nature had won out.

Unfortunately, there is no such thing as safe sex with a were-wolf and the two had not been as careful as they should have been. Lon contracted lycanthropy, the spiritual impulse that produces a werewolf, and Nancy had, as she put it, 'freaked out'. She had gotten him through his initial Changes and had begun training him, but she felt out of her league since it had been so long since her own training.

I could have simply turned them over to the Guild Warriors, known to the Otherside as the magical police force, brushed my hands off and be done with it but I did not feel the need to ruin both of their lives. Instead, I spent a couple of hours briefing the young wolf on the essentials of the Charter and then sent the couple off to study with my friend, Michael Taylor, alpha of a small pack that operated out of the Wizard's College. I would have to follow up and make certain that the two appeared but I felt that the case was well resolved.

A very relieved Nancy Sanderson and her mate departed shortly thereafter, and I bid the owner of The Spot good night as I moved back out onto Chippewa. My phone had buzzed while I was in my confab with the two werewolves so I pulled it from my pocket and checked it, noting that I had a voicemail.

I sighed. It had been a couple of weeks since I had gotten out for a good run in the forest and I was overdue but it seemed that duty called. Sometimes, having two employers was not to my advantage.

I pressed the necessary buttons and listened as the message spooled up. A woman's pleasant alto voice with a hint of a British accent filled my ear. "Mr. Collins, my name is Amber Morgan. Joe Regal gave me your name and suggested I call you. I am working on an . . . interesting case right now and wonder if I might consult with you. Could you please give me a call back when you get this message?" The caller left her number and hung up.

I glanced at my watch and realized that it was much too late to be making business calls. I would have to call Amber Morgan in the morning but, in the meantime, there was someone I could call. I opened my contacts, scrolled through, and punched up a number. The phone burred in my ear several times before a whiskey baritone answered. "Regal."

"Joe," I said, "Zach Collins. Just got a call from an Amber Morgan who says you recommended me. What's up?"

Regal, like myself, worked for Greenwood Resources Inc., a detective agency specializing in the recovery of missing children. GRI was run by a real, honest to god prince of the Daoine Sidhe so our efforts covered young ones from both sides of the Veil. "You know who Amber is, right?"

I nodded to myself. "Sure, she runs Buffalo Paranormal Investigations. I've heard good things about her."

"Yeah, Amber is good people. I went to high school with her and I've helped her out on a couple of cases. Don't want to spoil the reveal for you but she has a case, hostile haunting, that has elements that have Black Dog written all over it," Regal said in a matter-of-fact voice.

People who work for GRI are fully read in on the Charter so Joe was one of few humans who knew what I actually was. "How so?" I asked.

"Well, the pics I have seen from Amber's crew look a hell of a lot like a were."

My ears perked up. "You think there is a rogue in the area?"

"Nah. Whatever it is, it is definitely a spirit but the pics made me wonder if this was not the ghost of a werewolf."

I considered that for a moment. "Well, that would be unusual, wouldn't it? Okay, I will give her a call in the morning and see what's what."

"Thanks, I've got two cases working at once right now and, unlike you and his highness, I actually need to sleep."

We both laughed as I hung up. One of the reasons that I held two jobs was that, under normal circumstances, I do not require a lot of sleep. It was 'suggested' to me, by the Black Dog Council, that I find something more to occupy my time than simply hunting rogues.

Right now, though, I was more than ready for that run in the woods I had been considering earlier. I climbed into my Scion xB, lovingly nicknamed the Xbox, and headed south.

CHAPTER TWO

I woke late the next morning, after a long run in the woods of the Seneca reservation, and stretched languorously on my king- sized bed. I hopped carefully off the bed, claws ticking on the wooden floor of my living quarters.

I stopped in front of the full-length mirror to the right of my bed and regarded my doggy reflection for a moment. In my human form, I am a little over six feet, lean with dark hair and eyes. I think the Black Dog form is much more impressive.

If you think of an extremely tall Irish Wolfhound, turn the hound glistening jet black and make it more massive through the shoulders and jaws, you begin to get a vision of my hound form. Add black eyes, like the void of space, that glow with a sullen red light when I am on the hunt or using magic and the picture is complete. I suppose I am not surprised that humans call us Hell-hounds, even though I have nothing to do with the infernal realms.

I huffed a deep sigh, reached within, and turned my form inside out, reverting to the human-seeming. Unlike a werewolf, who can take as long as half an hour for the Change, my native magic makes it simple for me to move from one form to the other and, while I am a Black Dog, it is difficult for me to carry on business in that form. Since I had wrapped up my rogue case last night, my first order of business this morning was to contact Amber Morgan.

I threw a robe on and wandered over to the kitchen counter where I had left my phone charging the night before. I listened to Morgan's message once more then hung up and dialed the number she had given. My potential client answered within two rings. "Buffalo Paranormal Investigations. This is Amber."

"Ms. Morgan, this is Zach Collins. I am returning your call from last night."

Her voice warmed a touch as she recognized my name. "Mr. Collins, thanks so much for calling me back. Joe Regal suggested that you might be able to assist me with a case I have been working on."

As it turned out, Amber Morgan was not available to meet until the afternoon so I asked her to send me whatever her team had gathered. If I had not been known to Joe, I had a distinct impression that she would have turned me down flat but, after a bit of hesitation, she agreed to forward her case notes, interview recordings and video to my secure GRI email account. We agreed to meet at two that afternoon at One Seneca Center.

True to her word, the head of BPI began forwarding email almost as soon as we had hung up and I began my homework for the case.

At first, the case information did not seem that unusual to me. The Frederickson's, Colm and Marie, along with their son Marcus had moved into an old farmhouse south of Buffalo near the Pennsylvania State line. They had experienced incidents typical of a haunting: objects seeming to disappear and reappear in other locations, doors closing on their own, the feeling of being watched and seeing movement from the corner of the eye.

The files did not get interesting until I began to read Marcus' testimony, expertly pulled from him by Amber. The boy's experience was quite a lot worse than his parents. During his first day in the house, he had seen what he called a big dog and had even drawn the paranormal group a picture of a huge gray thing with jaws dripping. Marcus had been plagued by bloody nightmares, another apparition that he called, the bent over man, and scratching sounds coming from outside his bedroom window. BPI had included pictures the father had taken of the gouges in the siding outside the son's window and given the apparent size of the marks, I began to understand why the family was so concerned.

In addition to the focus on Marcus, there had also been unexplained howling around the property and the family had found blood on the front porch twice and a large unidentified canine track. Law enforcement had verified that it was animal blood; the family did not take much solace in this.

Perhaps the most interesting piece of evidence in the case files, though, was video taken by one of the BPI investigators while they were doing a visit at the property. Marcus had begun to grow agitated as they were speaking with him and then gestured toward his window. BPI had begun rolling video immediately and had caught a flicker of motion passing by. The group gave chase and came out into the front yard in time to capture about fifteen-seconds of a strange gray shape disappearing into the tree line.

I began to see why Joe had gotten Amber in touch with me; it was possible that I was suffering from pareidolia but the gray figure in the video certainly appeared to be a werewolf in mid-shift.

I took a break to let the case simmer in the back of my mind, bathed, and gorged on a couple of raw steaks I had thawing in the fridge. Unlike the omnivorous werewolf, a Black Dog is purely carnivorous.

As I was shifting my jaw back into a more human form, my phone rang. I picked the device up and answered. "Collins."

Even in my human form, I have extraordinarily sharp ears but I did not need them to hear the stress in Amber's voice. "Mr. Collins. I've just had some news that makes the case I sent you more urgent. I wonder if we could move our meeting up?"

"Tell me what is happening," I responded in what I hoped was a calming tone.

"Marcus was leaving for school this morning. Something attacked him and he fell off the stairs and broke his arm." My eyebrows shot up. Ghosts can be hostile, of course, but, despite the reality shows, an attack was a rare event.

"What sort of something, Ms. Morgan? Did this seem to be a physical entity or something more on the ghost side?"

"Ghost side, from what Marcus and the parents told us. They all saw it and said that it looked like the apparition that we caught on the video."

I nodded to myself, relieved that I was not dealing with a rogue werewolf. "Are the Frederickson's back at the house?"

"Oh no," the ghost hunter replied, "I picked them up at the hospital and have them staying at a safe place until we can investigate and find out what's going on."

"Probably not a bad idea. Rather than moving the meeting up, why don't you give me a chance to finish looking through the files and we can make a run up there this evening."

The BPI investigator seemed to consider this for a moment then responded affirmatively. She gave me the address to her home in an expensive area along Elmwood and we agreed to meet there at four that afternoon.

I finished the final bits and pieces of the BPI files and checked in with Janice Arai, the second in command at GRI, to make sure that she had me logged as 'on a case' for her records. Janice is easy to get along with as long as you understand that things will be done her way. Given that she is a nine-tailed kitsune beneath her human glamour, neither I nor anyone else at GRI, including the boss, argues with her. The nine-tailed are in a magical weight class all their own and this nine-tail also happened to be an expert martial artist.

* * *

I PULLED into the driveway of Amber's lovingly restored Victorian home at precisely 4:00 and the lady of the house was already on the porch to greet me. Getting out of the Scion, I realized that Joe Regal had failed to warn me that Amber Morgan was drop dead gorgeous.

From the dark red hair that cascaded in a ponytail halfway down her back to the natural flush in her cheeks, this woman was born to wear the colors of autumn and, as she moved down off the porch to greet me, I noted that she moved with the unconscious poise and centered gait of one who has years of physical training. I wondered to myself whether she was a dancer, a martial artist or both.

She stopped just short of the car and waited for me to exit before stepping forward and offering her hand. "Mister Collins, I appreciate your quick response."

I gave her hand a firm shake and smiled my most professional smile. "Please feel free to call me Zach."

The beautiful redhead returned my smile but there was a certain wariness to it. "Zach, then," she said, "please call me Amber. Did you have any questions about the case files I sent you?"

I shook my head. "You and your team keep excellent records. I feel that I am very much up to speed."

"And did you want to talk to my clients before we leave?" Amber asked, watching for my reaction.

I shook my head. "I have a good feel for them from the notes and I see no reason to bother them now. I do not want to get hopes up, honestly, so I would rather go see what can be done and present them with good news if I can."

"And how do you propose to help them, Zach? Joe told me you were the guy for this but he was not very specific."

I kept my face bland. "Why don't we talk about that along the way. It is getting late."

Amber glanced at her watch and looked up at me then cocked her head oddly. "Yes, I suppose we had best get going then. The sun will be down a little before seven tonight. No need to hunt ghosts in the dark." She switched gears abruptly, "Do you mind if we take my car? I have some equipment I would like to take for tonight's investigation."

I did not see any reason to demur so I shrugged and gave an affirmative response. Amber went back in the house for a moment and, before too long, the garage door at the side of the house opened and a silver Chrysler mini-van rolled out.

I hopped up into the passenger seat of the vehicle and my new client maneuvered the vehicle down to the end of her drive and into traffic. It did not take long for us to navigate downtown Buffalo and then move through the freeway system to the 90.

CHAPTER THREE

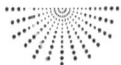

*T*he drive to the Frederickson farmhouse was quite pleasant once Amber and I got past the sticky question of how I was supposed to help her clients. Charter regulations are very specific; one does not talk about the Otherworld and its denizens with humans. There are some exceptions to that rule but, suffice to say, I could not simply tell Amber I was a Black Dog, that I have a native power for working with the dead and that there was a very good chance that I could send whatever was haunting the Frederickson's off to the afterlife.

After a little verbal evasion on my part, Amber turned her piercing green eyes from the road to me for a moment and exasperated, said, "Zach, I have worked with Joe on several cases. I swear he called in a wizard or exorcist or something for one of our hostile hauntings. Fellow came in, ran us out of the house, there was a flash of golden light and no spirit when we went back in. This fellow would not say squeak to me either and Joe told me that there are rules that must be abided by. I understand and respect that but you cannot fault me for being curious."

I smiled and shook my head. "No, I get it. Let's just say that I have to be very careful about what I say, for my protection and yours."

She regarded me out of the corner of her eyes but held silence so I continued, "I have been doing this sort of thing for a long time. I am not a medium—I do not simply throw the doors open to whoever or whatever happens to be around—but I do have a certain facility with the dead and ability to get them to go on to wherever they belong. So, I am hopeful we can get your 'bent over man' to move along with minimal fuss."

Amber nodded, flicking a glance at me before setting her eyes back on the road. "Okay," she said, extending the syllables, "fair enough. So, can you tell me about some of the cases you have worked on?"

The rest of the long drive along the shore of Lake Erie was spent 'swapping lies', as the humans say. I told some very expurgated tales of my encounters with spirits and some detective stories about tracing missing kids and Amber doled out some funny stories about her first ghost hunting cases and then the more serious spirit incursions she had seen. By the time we took the exit to Ripley, grabbed the 76 toward Lake Erie and then got on the 5, we were getting along famously and I found myself wishing I could get to know this beautiful and charming woman better.

I shook my head and thrust those thoughts firmly aside. Dating a human, even casually, was not a luxury I could afford. And I suspected that any relationship with Amber Morgan would go beyond casual very quickly.

* * *

THE FREDERICKSON FARMHOUSE was an old two-story clapboard structure with windows aplenty and French doors peeking out of the side of the home, presumably leading into one of the bedrooms. A narrow porch wrapped around three sides of the house and I could see that Colm was in the process of repairing some of the railing. The house was surrounded by a well-kept lawn that gave way, about two-hundred-feet from the house to the mixed oak, aspen, birch, and maple forest common to Western New York. Trees grew tall around three- quarters of the house, only giving way in the spot where the original farmers had placed their fields.

I opened the van door and eased myself out, stretching my legs after the drive. Amber followed suit and moved quietly around the front of the minivan to join me. It was almost completely silent; the ticking of the cooling engine was the only sound that reached my ears. No scurrying of small animals in the undergrowth, birds singing in the trees or dogs barking in the distance.

"Stay close," I murmured to Amber, "something is off kilter."

Amber nodded and whispered, "Way too quiet. This place is normally hopping at night . . . unless our friend is around."

That was when the smell hit me. Werewolf. I didn't think; I grabbed Amber around the waist and moved her as quickly as I could behind the van. The smell had wafted in from the tree line where the garden field gave way to the woods and I wanted to put something solid between the human and anything that was going to come at us.

Most women would have fussed at being manhandled but, when I released her, Amber only crouched and looked hard at me. She wanted an explanation but some part of her was also aware of the danger.

A rogue werewolf should have charged but, if this was a wolf, its behavior had been atypical. I had never heard of a werewolf harassing the same person or groups of people for any length of time without there being a bloody attack.

I popped my head over the hood of the van and gazed at the

woods, where the scent had come from. Being sure that Amber could not see my eyes, I tapped the fire within me and really looked. In my inner vision, the forest lit up with all manner of nature spirits but none of them seemed to have the slightest interest in Amber and me, and none of them had the fiery red, heated aura of a werewolf.

I pulled back on my power and rose slowly, ears tuned to the slightest sound of an intruder. Silence still reigned although now I was aware of the buzzing and faint songs of the tree spirits as they made their rounds. Amber slowly unfolded from behind the van as well. "Okay, what was that about?" she queried as her eyes quartered the lawn in front of her.

I could still smell a faint hint of werewolf but I could not see him anywhere. I wanted to get my client inside the house where she could be more easily protected if I were wrong. "I guess I overreacted after hearing about Marcus. I thought I saw something moving toward us when I got out of the van and didn't want to take any chances."

Amber considered me for a moment. "Okay." I could tell from her expression that she was thinking about just how quickly I had gotten her under cover. She held her tongue and followed me as I moved slowly away from the van.

We got about halfway from the van to the front door when the thing burst out from under the porch. My arcane senses told me that it was a spirit; my nose told me it was a werewolf and my common sense told me it was dangerous. It lunged for Amber as she ducked to one side, and I was astonished to note that she could see the spirit clearly.

I did not have time to consider that. I barked the shield rune, Algiz, covered Amber with it and poured my will into the magic as the spirit rounded to make a second pass. Amber's eyes widened as I dropped the shield on her; she had to be psychic and knew that I was going to have some fancy explaining to do when this was over.

The spirit turned on me. Like the picture of the bent man apparition in the BPI files, this spirit had the appearance of a man in the process of the Change. Without the stoop, he would have been average height but with his back bowed he more closely resembled a simian than a human. His face had the pulled out, elongated look of a lycanthrope about to bring forth its snout. His hands were curled, the fingernails already lengthening into claws. The creature turned to me, snarling, its ruff erupting around its head and I refrained from snarling back.

My power flared within me and I looked the spirit directly in the eyes, bringing that magic to bear on him. "Stop," I commanded.

I didn't need a rune charm to bring this being to heel . . . he was dead already.

The spirit froze and I felt reasonably safe dropping the shield around my client. She came slowly to my side, staring at the creature that I held bound.

She looked at me sharply, "I'm guessing that you know what this," she gestured at the spirit, "is?"

I shook my head. "Not a clue but I can tell you that it's definitely dead."

She quirked an eyebrow at me. "And how would you know that?"

I decided to ignore the underlying question. "Well, I did tell you that I have a way with the dead. I wouldn't have been able to stop this fellow so easily if he wasn't dead."

My client looked searchingly at me. "I see. And if he hadn't been dead?"

I shrugged. There was little point in lying. I was already going to be in trouble with the powers that be when I filed my report on this incident. "Could have still stopped him but it would have taken a little longer."

Amber gestured at the spirit. The half wolf, half man spirit was beginning to waver. It takes a lot of energy for one of the dead to manifest itself in the Midlands. The spirit wolf returned my stare, glaring fiercely at me as it faded back toward the Other Side. That just wouldn't do. I poured my will down the connection between us and the ghost stabilized. "No going back. We're going to have a little conversation."

The being snarled at me in return. I sighed, very conscious of Amber standing close by my shoulder, but kept my focus on the ghost. "You need to understand something, spirit. I can make you answer. I would rather not do that but you will speak with me."

The creature growled low and lunged at me. I forced some energy down the link and the ghost fell to its knees, snarling as it rolled away from me. Amber placed a hand on my arm, as if to restrain me, but I didn't dare take my attention from the creature. "Not to worry," I said quietly, "you can't really hurt a ghost but most don't like to be restrained."

Amber stepped slightly away from me and it was only then that I realized she was shaking. "I can't say that I blame them. I have had close encounters before but this is way past even my definition of ordinary."

"Not trying to freak you out. I had no idea that this fellow was going to be so eager to greet us. I figured that we would come in, do some ghost hunting stuff, I could sneak in a little magical summons and have a talk with some half visible thing that wouldn't constitute a threat."

She nodded slowly, taking a deep breath, and visibly centering herself as the ghost settled down on its haunches, glaring at both of us. To my surprise, the spirit spoke, its voice a sullen rasp. "Enough of these games. What do you want of me, necromancer?"

Amber's breath caught and I realized that she could not only see the spirit, she could hear it. She seemed less interested in my being a necromancer than she was in the spirit. She turned to the ghost. "What the hell are you?"

The spirit turned burning eyes on her but seemed to dismiss

her from its mind, turning back to me. I was tempted to let Amber handle the interrogation just for that. I could see her bridle at the dismissal but I did not have time to be concerned about her feelings; this spirit was obviously hostile and I needed all my concentration for dealing with it.

CHAPTER FOUR

I turned a glare on the ghost wolf and said, in a voice
approaching a growl, "The lady asked you a question,
spirit. Answer her." I twisted the knot of power that held him and
he writhed on the ground.

After another fruitless struggle and a shot of energy to keep
him on this side of the Veil, he replied. "What do you think,
necromancer? What do I look like?"

I was getting tired of the attitude. I came close to an eye flare
as I spoke, emphasizing each word, "Answer the question."

The ghost flinched at the power in my voice and said hastily,
"Wolf. I am a wolf."

I nodded. "But you had a human form as well?"

The spirit nodded sullenly. I could hear Amber's sharp inhala-
tion as she realized what we were dealing with. "Are you telling
us that you are . . . were a werewolf?"

"Brilliant," the creature sneered, turning its gaze to me again.
It flicked its ears at the beautiful redhead, "What are you doing
with this mundane, necromancer?"

I shook my head and instead asked the question that most
needed answering. "Why are you here?"

The spirit seemed to shrivel in on itself. "In life, I was called George. George Calder. I cannot remember my home," it said with what almost sounded like a quiver in its voice, "but I know that it was close to here. I was killed, like this," the spirit continued, gesturing at its misshapen body, "near Tupper Lake in the Adirondacks."

"But you have not answered the question, spirit. Why are you in this place? Why do you continue to plague these people?"

The spirit dropped its head. "I am compelled."

My ears perked up. This might be a case for the Guild Warriors if this creature had been forced to haunt a residence by magical compulsion. "Who compels you?"

"The beast . . . killed me," it muttered.

"What beast?" I pressed. I had no idea how long Calder had been dead but anything powerful enough to kill a werewolf was definitely a threat that needed dealing with.

"Not what beast, idiot, the Beast."

I struggled to keep my mouth from falling open. "You were killed by the Beast?" That name only applied to one werewolf.

The ghost werewolf nodded. "He is here. In the mountains. And he waits."

A frisson ran up my spine and, even though Amber had little idea what we were talking about, I saw her straighten and look around nervously. "Why is he allowing you to tell me this, if it is truly he that compels you?"

The spirit wavered for a moment then clarified again. "He grows tired of hunting humans. He has lived long and he has grown bored. Now he longs for bigger, more challenging game," the spirit glared at me once more, "he seeks to challenge a Black Dog."

I nearly choked and knew that my face had shown some of what was going through my mind since even more tension crept into Amber's frame. The spirit, under my compulsion, could not lie. He truly believed that the Beast of Gevaudan, the most feared rogue werewolf of all time, the lycanthrope who had slipped through the jaws of any number of Black Dogs and who had left many of those Dogs critically injured in the process, was in my territory.

I admit it. My concentration slipped for a moment. I expect it would have happened to even a more seasoned Black Dog but I refuse to make excuses. As soon as he felt my hold on him waver the spirit wolf lunged straight for Amber. In my hubris, I had dropped the shield that I had thrown over the ghost hunter. Before I had time to react, the spirit wolf had clamped its jaws on her forearm. The iron tang of blood came to me as Amber uttered a cry of pain through clenched teeth.

I pulled hard from the fiery core of my center, targeted on the spirit, and bellowed the Hel rune, my will rising like a lash around me. Between the twin forces of my native ability with the dead and the powerful Word of the Norse goddess of the afterlife, the ghost wolf stood no chance. The magic I had unleashed caused Calder to disappear into the Other Side with an audible pop, as though he had been pulled through a narrow hole by an inexorable vacuum. I heard the faint echo of his howl of frustration and rage as he disappeared.

I turned back to my client who stood, cradling her arm, staring at the blood leaking from the bite. She turned hollow eyes on me then simply said, "How?" Then she fainted.

* * *

THE RECORDED instances of a human being bitten by the ghost of a werewolf are very few but, in the annals of the Black Dogs, such things were not unheard of. If the spirit wished to transmit lycanthropy, it could, and I had to assume that George Calder had been compelled to do just that. It was imperative that I find out before Amber returned to consciousness.

I touched her forehead and found that she was burning with

fever and then I pulled the injured arm to me and looked at the bite. The wound was already scabbing over. That and the high temperature were clear indicators that she had been infected but, just to be certain, I moved to her head and dropped to my knees in the wet grass. I took a deep breath and opened my sight to the realms outside of normal human perception. A faint reddish glow lit my client's face as my eyes lit from within and I looked at her with the gaze of a Black Dog.

At first, I could see nothing but the lovely face, limned in the hellish glow of my eyes but as I sank deeper and additional layers of reality began to make themselves apparent, I saw what I feared. Overshadowing the face of the woman before me was the pale image of a wolf. An image that was taking on shape and substance even as I watched.

I looked to the sky; to the half-moon peeking over the tree-tops and sighed, trying to decide how best to handle this new development. In a little less than two weeks, Amber Morgan would become a werewolf.

I waited another few minutes, allowing the calm of the yard and the surrounding forest to seep into my bones then placed my hands gently on each side of Amber's face. I sent a small shock of magical current through her and her eyes flickered open almost immediately.

"What the hell?" she muttered as she sat up slowly, shaking her head as though that would clear the cobwebs.

It took a moment for the confusion to clear and the events of the night to settle back into place. Amber looked down at her arm, which I had wrapped with a swatch of my t-shirt, and as practical a woman that she was said, "I'm going to need to see a doctor for this." Her scent and the modulation of her voice told me that she was deathly afraid but she was damned if she was going to let anyone see that.

I gestured at the bandage with my chin. "Take that off first."

She hesitated for a moment, wanting to ask me why but then

braced herself visibly and simply jerked the makeshift bandage down to her wrist. While there was some dried blood around the bite, new soft, pink skin had already grown in and the bite was well on its way to healing completely.

Shock, fear, and curiosity warred on the ghost hunter's face as she looked to me for an answer. I sighed deeply. I have never been an exponent of the break-it-to-them-gently school but I figured that how she got the news should be left up to her.

"This might seem like a silly question but bear with me. I can guess the answer but I want you to tell me: when you were a kid and you had to have a Band-Aid for some injury, were you one of those kids who ripped the Band-aid off quick or messed around with it for a while, pulling the edges up and trying to soak it off and such?"

My client looked at me as though I had gone quite mad. "I ripped it off," she replied in a voice that was steadier then she was feeling. "I thought so. So, you prefer to get things on the table and deal with them, right?"

She nodded, just a trace of fear showing in the tightening of the muscles around her throat.

"You realize that you have been bitten by the spirit of a were-wolf, right?"

She nodded again, her face neutral.

"Until today, you really didn't believe that werewolves existed. Am I right?"

For the third time she nodded, her eyes riveted on my face as though she might detect the joke at any moment.

"Amber, werewolves and a lot of the other creatures that you have only read about in books actually do exist. Lycanthropy is transmitted via a kind of spiritual impulse. In living werewolves, it is transmitted through bodily fluids so a bite or unprotected sex with a werewolf can transmit that impulse."

She held up a hand to stop me and I could see anger starting to kindle in her fever-bright eyes. "Let me guess. Now you are going to tell me that this spirit has transmitted this impulse to me and that I am going to become a werewolf, right?"

I knew the drill. Denial was the first order of business when an accidental infection occurred. "That's right."

I recognized the grace, elegance, and efficacy of White Crane Kung Fu as Amber came to her feet in one fluid motion and almost put me down with a flat handed push to the chest. "You are so full of shit!" she screamed, "What kind of demented joke are you trying to pull?"

I backed off a step to give her space. "No joke," I replied in an even voice, trying to keep her as calm as I could, given the situation, "right now you're running a fever and all of your joints hurt. It feels like you have a mild case of the flu. In a couple of days, those symptoms will go away and you will feel just fine. In fact, you will feel better than you have ever felt in your life. You will notice a sharpening in your reflexes and strength and your sense of smell and hearing will gradually improve past human levels. Then, the full moon will hit . . ."

Amber backed slowly away from me. "I don't know what your game is, Mr. Collins, but I'm not playing anymore. I'm getting in the van and driving to the nearest hospital to have this bite checked out. And you . . . can find your own way home."

I didn't try to approach her. I knew from experience that, with her reality reeling around her, she was going to be unpredictable and I didn't want to provoke another violent outburst.

"Amber," I said, as reasonably as I could, "I know this is a lot to take in all at once. What would you say if I told you that I could prove to you that things like werewolves exist?"

The ghost hunter stopped moving towards the van. There was a part of Amber Morgan that already knew the truth and it was struggling to assert itself. She didn't say anything—just stared hard at me—but I knew that I had hooked the curious ghost hunting part of her.

I raised both hands, palms up, and said quietly, "Here is the deal. You're welcome to go sit in the van. You can even put the keys in the ignition. All I ask is that you do not drive off without me until you see what I have to show you."

Amber stood still for several moments and then turned decisively to the van. She pulled the keys from her jeans pocket and eased herself into the driver's seat. She put the keys into the ignition and sat, waiting.

I moved out into the middle of the yard where she could see me in the full light of the moon. I did not want her to be able to rationalize later that it had all been a trick of the moving shadows of the trees around me. I shucked off my jacket and shirt before the ghost hunter had a chance to object and took a deep breath. Before I thought better of this idea, I reached into the fiery core of my being and turned my form inside out, Becoming that which I really am.

CHAPTER FIVE

*O*f course, it took me a little while to disentangle myself from the rest of my clothing but, by the time I had wriggled loose from the pants, Amber was standing next to the minivan, torn between her native curiosity and the desire to jump back into the vehicle and haul ass out of there. I approached her slowly and stopped a short distance away, giving her time to assimilate.

After a moment, she leaned back against the Chrysler and huffed out a breath that was half laugh and half gasp. "Zach?" she asked, still not quite believing what she had seen with her own eyes.

Now, it was time to seal the deal, as they say. I focused and touched her mind, "Yes," I replied softly, mind to mind.

Her eyes widened. "Okay. One more absolutely bizarre thing in a night full of lunacy." I started to reply to that but she went on. "Alright, I am faced with either being crazy as a loon or you are telling me the truth. I guess I will operate under the assumption that I have not lost my mind. For the time being, at least."

I cocked my head to the side and tried to look as friendly as a hellhound with glowing red eyes can. "You know folklore. What am I?"

She did not hesitate. "A Phantom Black Dog. Does that mean I'm about to die or something?"

I moved my head back in forth in the semblance of a head shake. "No. We do have power over the dead but we don't bring death with us."

Amber tried to chuckle but I could hear the tremor of near hysteria underneath. I moved up close to her and put my shoulder lightly against her hip. I might be a Black Dog but canids, even large ones, seem to have a calming effect on humans. Without thinking, Amber dropped her hand into the ruff of longer fur around my neck and held on tight. I reached out for her mind again, "Look, I know this is a lot to take in all at once. The best thing you can do right now is to try not to swallow the whole impossible pill all at once. We have a couple of weeks before the full moon . . ."

Her head came up slightly. "We?"

I dropped my head in what looked like a nod. "The Other Side is governed by something called the Charter. Sort of like the Constitution for supernaturalism. Almost all the major tribes of Other Side beings have signed on to the Charter . . . I will tell you more about the history later. Right now, all you need to know is that the Black Dogs are basically werewolf enforcement officers under Charter provisions. Since you have been infected as the direct result of working with me on a case, I am responsible for bringing you into our world and teaching you the rules."

Her back straightened and I could smell the acrid tang of her temper rising. "And what if I refuse? Seems to me you've done enough damage."

I laid my ears back in an expression of remorse. "I'm truly sorry, Amber. As I told you earlier, I had no idea what we were dealing with when we came out here or I would never have involved you. What is done is done though and refusal is not an option. If you will not work with me, then I will have to take you in to the Guild Warriors—um, sort of like the paranormal police officers—and they would place you in a pack where you would be trained whether you liked it or not. I know the local Alpha; I think you'll get along a lot better with me than with him."

The set of her shoulders was still belligerent. "I don't normally play this card but you do realize that my dad is Tyler Morgan, right? The real estate mogul? I have more money than I will ever need. I could just disappear."

I simulated a head shake. "No, you couldn't. There is nowhere on this planet that you can go where there isn't a Black Dog tasked with looking for rogue werewolves and that is what you would be. I would have to report you the second I got back to Buffalo and the search would begin. That's assuming you could even evade me. Do you really want to spend the rest of what will be a very long life being hunted?"

Amber considered this for a moment and then the anger seemed to drain from her. "No, I think I'm in enough trouble as it is. I . . . I just don't know how I'm going to do this. My work, my team, how am I going to live a normal life if I am going to go off my rocker with every full moon."

Now we were getting to the crux of the issue. "Look, it will be much easier to have this conversation if I Change back. Doing the telepathy thing is difficult for me."

Amber waved a hand at me. "Okay—I needed convincing; I am convinced. Let's talk properly."

I strode back over to my clothes. I considered just Changing but I knew that Amber hadn't had time to develop the werewolf's tolerance for nudity. "Unless you want a look at my backside, you might want to turn around for a moment."

The ghost hunter turned toward the van with disheartening alacrity and I Changed back into my human form. I pulled my clothes back on quickly and then said, "Okay. I'm dressed. It's safe to turn around."

She turned back and regarded me with new eyes. "I have to tell you—that's a little creepy."

I shrugged. "In a few months, you'll think nothing of it. Now, since this place is quiet and ghost free, why don't we go inside, see if the Frederickson's have a coffee pot and answer some of your pressing questions."

Amber gave her own disheartened shoulder shrug and followed me up the porch stairs and to the front door. She produced keys from the back pocket of her jeans and led the way into the cozy farmhouse.

* * *

AMBER and I spent the next couple of hours in the Frederickson's gigantic kitchen, drinking coffee, as I gave her the basic facts about werewolf life. She relaxed a little when I explained to her that she was not going to go off her rocker with every full moon but that she needed training so that she could bring forward the human mind during her Change. She was not thrilled to learn that she needed to Change on a regular basis to avoid feeling like a caged wolf in the city but I cushioned that hard truth with the knowledge that, once she had made it past that first full moon, she could choose when she wanted to Change so that she could adapt her unusual new life to fit her needs.

I laid out a couple of other hard truths for her: that werewolf females can't bear children and that, due to the regenerative effects of the Change she was now practically immortal. There was really no way to soften those blows and I needed to get them out there for her to work on but I won some points when she asked me what I thought the best thing about being a werewolf might be.

I answered her as candidly as I could. "I hear all kinds of things from my wolf friends but let me answer that from my own experience as a shapeshifter. Yes, our life in the Midlands—

this physical realm that we live in—can be pretty awkward at times. We have secrets that we have to keep because of the Charter and we have to respond to that deep inner call to run in our other form. We watch humans that we are fond of grow old and die while we remain young and vigorous and we have to be attentive to the dangers in this world as well as the Other Side. All of that really bites and I do not want to try to sweeten it for you."

"But, imagine if you will, what it might be like to run the woods on four feet?" I continued, "To smell every smell, to hear every sound, to lift your face to the moon and howl? Even certain human beings have the desire to be out in nature, to try to unite with it. Imagine what it would be like to truly be a part of it and yet to have the control and consciousness to bring those experiences back with you," I could hear her take a breath as I spoke.

"There is no way that any description I can give you can recreate that experience but in a couple of weeks, you will have that understanding. To me, that is the good stuff and it makes it worth all the strictures that we face in our human lives. For that time, you can be more truly free than any human can hope to be."

I glanced up into her face. Amber's eyes had gone from green to wolf gold as she contemplated what I was saying. "I think," she said in a husky voice, "that this is going to take some getting used to. But, it might not be so bad. When do we start?"

I laughed then, relieved that we were over the hump. I knew that, in the days to come, she would have her ups and downs but this basic acceptance that things might not be as bad as she thought was a good start. "It is well after midnight so first; we go catch some shuteye. We can talk more in the morning."

Amber and I got on the road after cleaning up the kitchen. My new student balked immediately when I told her that I was going to have to stay with her, more or less constantly, until I could get her through her first Change. And probably, for a while after that. She still didn't understand quite how tenuous her position was, that I was the only thing standing between her and the Guild Warriors, so I had to lay it out for her.

I think the idea of me hunting her as a rogue scared her worse than the idea of being turned over to the Guild Warriors. Eventually, she relented and, by the time we made the outskirts of the metro-Buffalo, we had agreed that I would take up temporary residence in her guest house once the Frederickson's had returned home.

By the time we made it back to the house on Elmwood, I was very glad that I had insisted on driving. Amber would never have admitted it but the sag to her shoulders, the puffiness around her eyes and the stiffness she evinced as she climbed out of the mini-van, told me that she was weary. Every werewolf that I had ever spoken to said that the first couple of days of the infection made them question their decision to come over to the Other Side. This new wolf needed rest and plenty of food and fluids to get her through the beginning phase of her new life.

As soon as we were in the door, I practically pushed her to the long staircase and ordered her to get some sleep. She didn't resist much; I watched her climb heavily up the stairs, after directing me to the guest bedroom and disappear down the hallway that presumably led to her sleeping quarters.

Now that I had attended to my Black Dog duties, it was time to touch base with my other employer.

CHAPTER SIX

I pulled out my cell and hit the speed dial. I held the phone to my ear; the line rang exactly once before it was picked up. The Sidhe do not require much sleep either. "Good evening, Black Dog. Given the hour, I assume this isn't a social call?"

"You would be correct. I expect Joe Regal has briefed you on the haunting case he sent my way?"

"Yes."

"Well, the case developed some major complications tonight and I may need GRI's support."

Al-lin of the clan Greenwood, Allan Greenwood in the human world, had known me since my days studying combat magic with the Sigrun of the Valkyrja. An exiled prince of the Daoine Sidhe, Al-lin often forgot that he was not still a prince of the realm and I considered it my personal duty to remind him. Despite the occasional slinging of barbs though, there were few beings in the Midlands or the Otherworld that I trusted more in a tight situation. I laid out the events of the night for him, in detail, and then stopped, waiting to hear his thoughts on the matter.

There was a pause as the Sidhe prince thought things through.

"So," he said at last, "tell me something about the Beast of Gevaudan. I know the short version of the tale but I imagine your people have quite a lot more information."

"The Beast", I began, "La Bête, as the French called him, is a werewolf named Louis Chastel. His brother, Jean, is credited with having slain the Beast during this rogue's first incursion in France. Actually, Jean helped Louis escape. He killed a large wolf in the forest of Gevaudan and proclaimed that he had slain the Beast."

"Everyone in the area was so strained with fear that there was a sort of hysterical reaction and Jean Chastel became a local hero. Of course, the depredations of the Beast stopped, since Louis slipped away in the resulting flood of adulation for his brother, and Chastel has gone on to claim lives all over the world."

"He has never stayed in one place for an extended period of time and he has learned to cover his tracks much more carefully. Our limited information is that he has managed to amass quite a fortune over the years, both by choosing rich people as victims and by using his abilities to commit high-end thefts. "

"The Black Dogs have been on his trail from the beginning," I continued, "but the Beast has been the wiliest opponent we have ever faced. He is the closest thing that my people have to a boogie man and he has grown in strength and skill with each confrontation we have had with him. He has come close to killing a couple of the Dogs who have faced him and has slipped the noose, so to speak, a dozen times."

"Unlike most rogues, he is extremely calculating and always looking to add new skills that give him an edge to his repertoire. We have known for some time about his interest in the Black Arts but, given what I saw tonight, I would have to say that the monster has added necromancy to his list now." I stopped, waiting for questions.

"And now he is in your demesne," Al-lin said simply.

"I can't be sure of that. What I would ask of you is verification. Please check with your resources in the Adirondacks and perhaps have Kevin Chen do some of his computer magic to see if there have been more than the normal numbers of disappearances in the area recently. Chastel has to eat, even if he is hunting larger prey, and we know that he prefers human game."

Al-lin considered this for a moment. "Given the possible danger to everyone in those mountains, I will be happy to do this. What if we discover evidence that your rogue may be in the Adirondacks?"

"Then, I will have to hunt him. I have the magic and I know this old wolf as well any Black Dog out there. I hope I can count on your support."

Al-lin sounded almost affronted. "A monster loose in the forest with a reputation for slaying humans? Of course, you will have our support."

I stopped short of thanking the Sidhe prince—bad form when dealing with the light elves. "That would be good, Al-lin of the Greenwood. I will look forward to hearing from you later today."

I flipped the phone closed and got into the bed, Changing as I dropped onto the comfortable mattress. Dogs are creatures of the present; the threat of the Beast would keep until the morning.

* * *

I woke abruptly and glanced over at the small digital clock on the nightstand. 4:30. My ears perked; someone was moving around the house. Quietly, I sniffed the air. The after scent of perfume, light and floral, hit my nose immediately followed by a subtler human musk that I knew immediately. Amber was up.

I found her sitting on the couch, staring blindly out the French doors into the darkness beyond. She hadn't been a werewolf long enough to see anything in that darkness but the tautness of her frame under the billowy sleep shirt and the slight rocking of her body told me everything I needed to know. I whined softly to let her know I was there and she started, looking at me.

Her eyes were filled with tears, reflecting the fire of my eyes in the dark. "Hello, Zach. Damn, I was hoping that this whole night was a bad dream and I would wake up to find everything back to normal."

I moved slowly toward her. Once denial has been breached and there is some acceptance of the situation, most involuntary lycanthropes go through a fear stage. I eased myself forward and put my chin on her bare thigh. As before, she folded her fingers into the soft ruff of fur around my neck and then without warning flung her arms around me and buried her face in my pelt.

She still had hold of my ruff and was alternately trying to shake me and hug me at the same time. I stood still as she sobbed raggedly into my shoulder, waiting for her to calm a little before I tried to touch her mind. She didn't need words at that moment; she just needed my presence and I sought to emanate as much calm and reassurance as I could.

After a few minutes, she had cried herself out. She sniffled and drew away from me, casting about her for a Kleenex or something else to wipe her face and nose with. After a moment, she simply pulled up the edge of her nightshirt and cleaned her face with it. I stayed where I was, although I was acutely conscious that Amber was naked, except for her undergarments, under the sleep shirt.

When she had stopped hiccuping, and seemed to relax a little, I reached out for her. This time, the connection to her thoughts was easier, "I know you're scared. I grew up this way so I can't imagine what it's like to suddenly be faced with all this. All I can tell you is that I'm here for you and that is not just because of my duties under the Charter. I like you and I hope we can get past the anger that you must feel toward me and be friends."

I had not meant to start her crying again but I did. Again, I stayed still and let her sob herself dry on my shoulder. When she had finished her second bout of tears and used the poor sleep shirt again, she rose quietly and gestured for me to follow. I padded along behind her, back down the hallway to the guest bedroom. Amber flopped down on the bed, obviously exhausted, and patted the mattress next to her. I jumped up and settled myself cautiously next to her, unsure of her intentions. She snuggled herself up against my back, murmured, "No changing back 'til I leave the room," and promptly fell back asleep.

It had been a long time since I had shared a bed with anyone, in either form, and I had to resist the urge to move around. The warm length of the new werewolf against my back pulled my mind in directions that I couldn't act on in dog form so I banished those desires as they arose and quickly dozed back into a light but restful sleep. My dreams were quite pleasant.

* * *

AN HOUR LATER, I managed to get out of bed without disturbing the sleeping new wolf, Change and get cleaned up so that I could meet the Frederickson's and give them the good news that their house was ghost free. Amber had arranged for the family to borrow one of her vehicles and leave it at the hospital, where she had retrieved them the day before, for one of her team to pick up later.

I introduced myself to the pleasant couple and their young son as a member of Amber's team made certain that they were well fed for the journey and sent them on their way. As often happens, the family was so happy to hear that their problem had been solved that they did not ask a lot of questions about how that had been accomplished. Humans, as a rule, would really rather ignore what they cannot see; otherwise, those of us who live alongside them would have a much harder time staying within the bounds of the Charter.

Shortly after I had trundled the clients off in Amber's mini-van, my reluctant host came down the stairs slowly. She glanced at the door to the garage. "Are they off then?"

I nodded, taking her in with a glance. She had wrapped a bright blue chenille bathrobe over the sleep shirt of the night before but her feet were bare. Nothing short of a wasting disease was going to make her anything less than beautiful but her skin was paler than usual except for the flush at her cheeks. Her eyes were fever bright and she moved like a woman three times her age.

"Feeling pretty rough this morning?" I asked.

She nodded, not bothering to deny it. "Felt worse. Once. When I had pneumonia in college that almost killed me. Thought my dad was going to call in the entire staff of the Mayo Clinic before I turned the corner."

I almost chuckled at that but held my peace. "You need to get some fluids in. Tea?"

She looked at me as though I were speaking a foreign language. "At this time of day? My dad was British, I am not. Give me coffee or get out."

I smiled and simply went into the kitchen to pour her a cup. When I returned with a steaming mug in my hand, she had seated herself on the couch with her feet curled underneath her. She took the coffee with a grateful half-smile but stopped me with a hand on my forearm before I could move away. "About last night . . ."

"I'm not making anything of it. It's very common for someone involuntarily infected to feel fear, especially in the night. You needed comfort and I was there in all my furry glory. I hope it helped."

Amber continued to look at me. "Yes, it helped. I normally have no trouble sleeping alone but last night . . ."

I took her hand and squeezed it. "Last night, your whole world changed. I would expect you to be a little off balance."

Her gaze was so intent that I almost looked away but somehow, I knew that would be the wrong thing to do. "I . . . last night you said that you hoped we would be friends."

I did look away then. "I know that is a lot to ask; I really blew it last night and you are paying the price. I am hoping you will forgive me, at least."

"I don't think that staying mad at you is an option. There is something that I have not told you."

CHAPTER SEVEN

I gave the new wolf a quizzical glance and she took a deep breath before going on. "Normally, this is not something I share with anyone but given my 'unusual' situation now, I figure that I need to be forthcoming. There is no easy way to put this but . . . I hear a voice in my head sometimes."

"A voice?" I queried, "Singular?"

Amber nodded, her pale cheeks coloring slightly with embarrassment, "Almost all my life, I have heard a lady talking to me. I have considered that I was schizophrenic but this voice tells me things and they are always, and I do mean always, correct."

"Does the voice have a name?" I asked, more curious than concerned. Amber Morgan struck me as being one of the most mentally stable people I had ever met.

The color rose ever higher in her cheeks. "She claims to be the goddess Hekate and she told me last night, as I was going to sleep, that I needed to stick with you despite all that has happened."

I struggled to keep my facial expression neutral. Hekate was a goddess known for traveling with ghosts, restless spirits, and dogs. It was said, in Ancient Greece, that her presence was heralded by the barking of all the dogs in a neighborhood. I was not certain whether to be frightened or honored by her confidence in me.

"Well, that changes things a little," I said after a moment, "I would have to do some psychic work with you but it seems that you might be what we call an Oracle—a being that can literally act as the voice of some deity or other Power. "

Amber stopped for a moment to digest that information and then asked, "How does that change things?"

"I can't be sure until you get past this flu stage but your unwitting connection to the Otherside will likely cause you to come into your abilities more quickly. Better sense of smell and hearing, increased night vision and the other things we talked about."

My new student nodded slowly. "Okay," she said, drawing the word, "something to look forward to."

"It really is not so bad once you get through your first Changes. Now, drink your coffee. You need to stay hydrated while we wait for this incipient phase to pass."

Amber nodded slowly, bringing the mug to her nose, and inhaling with apparent delight before taking a sip and smiling with evident satisfaction. A woman after my own coffee-loving heart.

* * *

MY NEW STUDENT and I spent the remainder of the morning going over the same basics I had covered with young Lon Giffords. Amber might have felt like hell but she proved to be an apt and eager student. She listened carefully, asked questions when she did not quite understand a point and urged me on, even when I thought she should be resting.

I did finally get her to go upstairs for a nap at a little past 11:00 by the simple expedient of threatening to sing lullabies to her in my native tongue if she did not. I sat and listened as she flopped on the bed in frustration and promptly stopped moving. I could hear the deep slow breathing of sleep filtering down the staircase moments later.

I pulled out my cell and noted that I was going to have to charge it soon. I needed to get to my place to pick up some clothes soon so I put the cell phone charger on my mental list. I hit a number in my speed dial and checked with the registrar's office at the Wizard's College to make sure that Mr. Giffords and his mate had shown up to register. I was relieved to find that they had indeed arrived and were in class as I spoke. That made my life easier. The last thing I needed right now was a rogue werewolf to track down. If the Beast were actually in the mountains to the east of me, I was going to be leading a very busy life for the foreseeable future.

Once I had hung up with the College, I considered checking in with Al-lin to see if he had heard anything yet. I was about to decide that it was too early for him to know anything when the phone in my hand buzzed. I checked the display and it was Kevin Chen's office number. I swiped to answer the call. "Collins."

"Zach, Al-lin here and I have Kevin Chen with me on speaker."

"Hi, Zach," another cheery voice chimed in. Kevin Chen was GRI's resident computer genius, a wiry Chinese man who had taken his PhD at MIT and gone on to do post-doctoral work at Carnegie Mellon and later CIT but had come to work for GRI when we recovered his missing daughter from a greedy bogie that had decided his Court was not providing him with enough high-quality protein. Chen had been invaluable to GRI; his skill in analyzing data and his ability to get into systems others could not had served us well on many occasions. "Morning, Kevin. Al-lin keeping you in good coffee?"

The computer expert laughed. I had never seen him in a bad mood, even in the thick of a desperate hunt for some missing person, but Kevin Chen loved coffee like I loved raw meat. "Oh, yeah. He got me some stuff from the Seelie Court in the Netherlands last week. To die for."

I smiled despite my tension. "Well, I owe you something for this job. I can't get that fancy but I will see what I can find over at The Spot."

I could hear the smile in his voice as the Chinese man responded, "Deal."

"I have some results from a search I have been running for you, per Al-lin's request. I have accessed data from the National Forest Service, State Parks, as many local law enforcement agencies as I could bring up, fire departments, any agency in the Adirondacks that might receive reports of missing persons. Seems that there has been a statistically significant increase in the number of unsolved disappearances in the area over the summer and into early fall."

"How significant, Edward?"

"Well, it is hard to give an exact number but I factored for people who just walk away, hikers who get lost in the woods, expire and are not found immediately, that sort of thing. Even factoring in as many reasons as I could think of, we still have a fifteen to 20 percent jump in disappearances since about March."

"Hell," I said, emphatically, "that did not happen by accident."

"No," Al-lin said, taking over from Edward, "and my contacts in the field tell me a similar story. People are starting to band together and not hike alone, there is an increase in firearm-related charge in the area as people are going armed more often, despite the law, and there are the inevitable conspiracy theories starting to cook— aliens, Bigfoot, monsters of all sorts. Some of them are surprisingly close to the mark."

"So," Al-lin continued, "I checked with the Sasquatch tribe near my cabin on the reservation. They owed me a favor after I managed to release one of their little ones from a steel trap some imbecile placed along Little River creek.

"What did the Sasquatch have to say?"

I could hear a grim edge creep into his voice. "Their cousins in the mountains have gone deep into the woods and stayed there. Apparently, they keep talking about the old monster in their forest and what a threat it is to their people. Even something as large and powerful as an adult Sasquatch is not going to take chances with a fanged, clawed menace like a werewolf. Given the disappearances and the Sasquatch reaction, I would say it is a pretty good guess that your Beast or some other fearsome rogue is loose up there. I have a human agent checking newspapers and the like but I wanted to get this to you as soon as possible."

I was glad I was sitting down. The statistics and the Sasquatch said I was going up against something nasty. Thinking of the Beast, my knees felt a little weak and it was not all excitement. "I appreciate that, Al-lin. Let me know when you have anything further. Especially if it gives me a place to start looking."

"I will do so. You realize that this falls into my purvey as well, correct?"

I frowned, "How so?"

The grim edge became sharp steel as Al-lin replied, "Some of the lost ones are children, Zachary. If this is what we think it is, you have GRI's full resources at your disposal and any other help you need. I won't go mucking about in your business; I know you are the expert but you have only to ask and I will do what I can to help."

"I appreciate that, Al-lin of the Greenwood, and so do my people. You can bet that I will ask when I need assistance."

"See that you do, Black Dog, see that you do," the elven prince replied and then hung up the phone.

* * *

I NEARLY JUMPED out of my skin when, a short time later, Amber asked if I were okay. I had been so deep in thought that I had not heard her come down the stairs. She reached over the back of the couch and laid a hand on my shoulder. "I'm sorry; I didn't mean to startle you."

I tried not to pay attention to the hand gently resting on my shoulder. "My fault," I responded, "I was doing some deep thinking. It's not normally so easy to sneak up on a Black Dog."

Amber came around the couch and sat down opposite me, shifting her robe to cover the taut lean leg beneath. I shook myself inwardly and looked steadfastly at her face.

My charge looked better after her nap. Her eyes were still a little too bright and her cheeks still showed too much color but she did not look like she was about the break into pieces as she settled herself. "Feeling better?" I asked.

The ghost hunter nodded. "I took some ibuprofen before I went to rest and that seemed to help," she shifted subjects quickly, "so, what is bothering you?"

CHAPTER EIGHT

I had already read Amber into the basics of life under the Charter and introduced her to the major players in the Midlands— wizards, the Fae, werewolves, and the occasional vampire—so I jumped straight to the most pressing issue. "I know that we have been very focused on what is going on with you in the past hours but I have another concern as well. The reason that I am here, taking the lead on educating you as you come up to the Change is that I am bound by the Charter to do so."

Amber opened her mouth to say something but I continued quickly, "I would have taken care of your education out of my sense of duty anyway, but the Charter is very clear that, if someone is Turned in the presence of a Black Dog, that Dog is responsible for the new werewolf until the Dog can be certain that the new one is not going to represent a danger to humans."

I could see that Amber wanted to ask what happened to wolves who are a danger but I went on before I had to get into the middle of that serious topic. "Do you remember what that spirit was talking about, right before you were bitten?"

Amber's brow crinkled in concentration. "Something about a beast and it wanting to challenge a Black Dog, right?"

I nodded. "Does that mean anything to you, O Loremaster?"

She grinned despite herself and looked down, accessing her knowledge of arcane lore. It did not take her long to put together the pieces of the puzzle. "Good God, he was not talking about the Beast of Gevaudan was he?"

I tried to keep it light. "Gold star."

Amber eyes me curiously, "But I thought Jean Chastel killed the Beast?"

"That is the party line in the story," I replied, "in reality; the Beast is a rogue werewolf named Louis Chastel. His brother, Jean, covered for him by killing an enormous wolf in the forest of Gevaudan and then claiming the wolf was the Beast. Louis slipped away and has become the most hunted rogue in Black Dog history."

"You mean, he is still running around? None of your people have been able to bring him in?"

I shook my head. "Chastel is wily and he has studied various kinds of magic over the years. He learned from Gevaudan that staying in one place for too long results in too much attention and makes it harder for him to take his prey. So, he will appear in a place for a few weeks or months, people will begin to disappear, mauled bodies will turn up, fear will rise in the area and, before it hits fever pitch, Chastel will move on."

Amber's face was serious as she looked at me. "And now the Beast has basically called you out?"

I raised my hands in uncertainty. "Maybe. Right now, I estimate that there is a good chance that Chastel is actually out in the mountains waiting for me—good but far from certain."

I could almost see ideas coming together in the ghost hunter's head. "Damn! So, basically, infecting me could be a way of hobbling you. You have to stay with me and teach me according to Charter regulations but you really need to be out in the Adirondacks hunting whatever is making people disappear."

I nodded slowly. "I have made a sort of a hobby of studying Chastel. Even if it is not him, it is the sort of devious thing that he would do."

Amber locked up at me and I was surprised to see fire in her eyes. "I am not going to allow that bastard to infect me and then use me to get you killed. It seems to me that we need to do something that will throw him off his stride."

I had been thinking much the same thing but had not come up with a good strategy yet. "Do you have something in mind?"

Amber grinned and I could see the wolf in it. "How long would it take you to turn me into a full-fledged werewolf?"

I opened my mouth to reply then closed it, uncertain what to say. After considering for a moment, I tried again. "Honestly Amber, I don't know. I've heard a couple of stories about the Change being accelerated but they're folklore. I would need to check with the people who trained me, the Valkyrja, to see what is truly possible."

Amber gestured with her head toward the kitchen. "You have a cell phone and there is a land line in there."

I could not help but chuckle. "The Sigrun, my magic teacher, does not have a landline. I have to use more arcane methods for contacting her." I looked at her frankly, "You're really serious about this?"

"Yes," she replied, "my father says that in many ways, I remind him of my late mother. Rule number one with her was: don't piss off the redhead. Whether you are dealing with Chastel or some other magical dirtbag, no one tries to use me as a pawn and gets away with it. I understand, from what you have said, that it takes years for a werewolf to come fully into her abilities but if I can't be a full member of the team then at least I can try not to be a complete liability."

I took a deep breath, held it for a moment then released it

slowly through my nose, giving myself a moment to consider. "Okay, I will see what I can find out. In the meantime, you need to get fully past the flu stage before we can do anything. Back to bed with you."

I thought she was going to argue with me for a moment but then she seemed to take stock of how she was feeling and change her mind. "Agreed. You will let me know as soon as you find out something?"

"Only if you're awake. I keep telling you that fluids and rest are the only way to get past the initial sickness."

Amber grumbled but went off to nap without too much further persuasion. Once I could hear the sounds of deep breathing coming from her sleeping quarters, I pulled out my phone and called Al-lin.

The head of GRI had further information for me. Kevin Chen's computer wizardry combined with some discreet inquiries from on the ground resources had confirmed that we were dealing with a rogue werewolf in the Adirondacks; the coroner's reports had shown the combination of bite marks consistent with a canine and deep scratches more in line with a feline that was the hallmarks of a werewolf attack. I asked if Al-lin had any news on where to begin my search and the elf prince put Kevin Chen on the phone. I did not follow the complex math but statistical analysis showed that the epicenter of the attacks was a place called Ampersand Lake in the High Peaks Wilderness. All the disappearances had occurred in slowly expanding concentric circles from that lake.

I asked Kevin to tell Al-lin to put one of our tactical teams on standby and then hung up. My next bit of conversation was going to require something more than a cell phone.

* * *

AFTER SIGNING OFF WITH KEVIN, I spent a few moments centering myself and listening carefully to make certain that my charge was still fully asleep. The sun was casting long golden beams across the yard outside the French doors by the time I felt ready to proceed.

I took a deep breath, let it out slowly and then took another, holding it for a moment before letting it go. Establishing a rhythm with my breath, I allowed my inhalations to become slower and softer and my consciousness, trained by hard practice, slowed and settled with my breath. Outside stimuli faded and the inner world opened to me.

I opened my inner eyes and found myself sitting quietly at the base of Yggdrasil, the World Tree, its massive roots towering over the little alcove I had chosen long ago for my safe spot on the Other Side. I sat for a moment, relishing the silence and the intense energy of life all around me, the dampness of the rich, loamy soil under my seat. If I had not had work to do, I would have taken some time to just sit. It is not often that one gets to relax at the very root of all existence.

I did have work to do; however, and, reluctantly, I set myself to call the Sigrun, Kara Grimsdottir, leader of the Valkyrja. I spoke the runes of her title slowly and quietly, not wanting to 'shout' an impolite call.

I did not have to wait long for the phantom figure of the Sigrun to appear before me.

Kara Grimsdottir was ancient. No one knew how old she was and no one who spent any time with her cared. Only the foolish disputed her strength and skill. She was tall, her posture straight despite her years and she had a face wrinkled into a roadmap of the wars and misery, laughter, and camaraderie she had seen. Clad in the gray hooded robe of her office, only twinkling blue eyes relieved the harshness of her expression and I could see that she was pleased to see me.

"The runes spoke of your coming and the need-fire burnt

amongst them. What brings you to seek counsel of an old woman, Black Dog?"

"The Beast, Mother."

The Sigrun stiffened. Many moons before this meeting, the Sigrun had predicted that my path would cross with Chastel's. It was one of the reasons that I had stayed with the Valkyrja training. "He has come?" the Sigrun queried, "You have seen him?"

"No, Mother, I have not encountered him yet, but it seems likely that I may." I spent a few minutes giving her a quick summary of all the information that I had while she gazed at me with ice blue eyes.

When I had done, she nodded and pulled open the deerskin pouch which hung at her waist. Muttering a quick prayer, she reached into the pouch and pulled forth a rune. She did not show me what she had drawn but looked at it for a moment with unfocused eyes, then dropped it back into the bag. "You and the elf are correct. 'Tis the Beast. The image that sprang to my Sight was Fenrir, the ravening one, and then the face of the one you call Chastel. I have considered sending one of the sisters out after the bastard wolf but was warned not to do so."

I nodded; my worst fears confirmed. "I have felt that it was Chastel almost since the beginning of this incident but I had hoped . . ."

"You fear him?" the Sigrun asked, blandly.

"Of course, Mother, I would be a fool not to."

The Sigrun nodded slowly. "It is good that you recognize your fear. In that way, it will not ambush you. I think though that you have not told me all of it. Why have you come to me, Hound of Hel?" I took a deep breath and explained the situation with Amber to her and Amber's idea about accelerating the Change. Her face clouded as I spoke and she shook her head when I was done. "It is not well to interfere with the Change. It can be done but very few come through with their sanity intact. She would have to be an exceptional human being for there to even be a chance for her."

During our conversations, I had learned something about Amber's martial arts training but my response still surprised me. "She is quite exceptional, Mother. She is trained as a warrior and she carries herself like one."

The Sigrun stopped to consider that for a moment, looking into the middle distance. I knew that look; she was working through a decision with the help of her Patron. I stood silent, waiting as expressions played across her face. At length, she turned to me and said, "That will help. If she has the necessary concentration, it is possible. I will want to meet this woman. Bring her to me when she has gotten past the sickness of being infected."

CHAPTER NINE

*W*hen I came to myself, the sun was almost fully set and I could hear Amber moving about in her bedroom. She came down the stairs shortly thereafter and I could tell right away, by her improved color and freer movement, that she was feeling considerably better. She still had circles of fatigue under her eyes but, true to my earlier supposition, she was moving through the incipient phase of her infection more rapidly than normal.

The infamous werewolf metabolism had kicked in and my new student was famished so we took the opportunity to feed her a couple of hefty burritos and a coke at a local Mexican place on Chippewa then drove over to my 'den' so that I could make a meal of the raw steak in my fridge and pick up some clean clothes.

I had a moment's awkwardness over my own dinner. In order to eat, I have to shift my jaw structure to accommodate my canine teeth. Amber had been exploring my warehouse apartment and emerged from her perusal of my Euro-style bathtub just as I began to eat. I stopped chewing in mid-bite and considered shifting my face back to its human form but it was too late for that. Amber walked slowly across the room to stand across the counter from me, her eyes locked on my elongated jaw, the wicked canines showing over my lip.

The new wolf took a deep breath and I could see her steady herself. After a moment, she asked, "May I touch?"

I knew that words would come out garbled with my jaw in the shape it was in. I just nodded, not sure what to expect in the next moment. Amber reached across the counter and ran a gentle hand down the long length of my mandible, cupping her hand under the point of my semi-muzzle. Her face was full of puzzlement and another emotion that I could not define.

"This may sound strange," the ghost hunter said, her voice soft, as though she feared that I might startle and bite, "but this actually looks natural on you. It's almost . . . handsome. Will I be able to do this when the Change comes?"

"Something like it," I garbled over teeth and mouth structure not designed for human speech.

Her green eyes looked deeply into my own and she smiled a fey smile. "You finish eating," she said, still cupping my muzzle, "I am sure I can find something else to look at to give you some privacy."

Once I had completed my meal, Amber clicked off the nature documentary she had been watching half-heartedly on my big screen television and joined me once more at the kitchen counter as I cleaned up.

I looked up at her as I finished wiping the counter and asked, "So, what is your question?"

My companion looked startled, as though I had just read her mind, and I laughed, "No psychic ability involved, honest. Remember when we talked about how hard it is to lie to a werewolf? Body language, heart rate and scent all come together to sort out a liar quickly. Your body language just about screamed that you were holding a question back."

Amber looked miffed for a moment but then smiled. "I am not

used to being read like a book; I've been told by more than one person that I have a good poker face. Anyway, what I wanted to ask you was, what did you find out about making the Change early?"

I smiled and regarded her beautiful face for a moment before I took a deep breath and replied, "You need to get a good night's sleep tonight. In the morning, we are leaving for Norway."

Of course, this pronouncement set off a tidal wave of questions from my curious new wolf. I did not want to flood Amber with too much information at once so swiftly brought the conversation around to the subject that I felt was most needful. "We can speak more in the morning but here is what I think you really need to know in order to make a decision about whether you want to go through with this."

My student eyed me cautiously and nodded for me to continue.

"I was born a Black Dog and had been through the Academy when I went to train with the Valkyrja and I was still scared witless. They have an awesome reputation in magical circles. In some ways, going in cold, coming from the human world will work to your advantage."

"First thing to remember about the Valkyrja: they are warriors. Every single member of the sisterhood is trained and very capable. I have already told the Sigrun, the leader of the Valkyrja, that you are a warrior so expect them to test you before they will even consider helping you."

Amber frowned. "Test me how?"

I returned her look steadily, "White Crane teach you anything about defending against a spear?"

The new wolf shrugged expressively. No martial artist worth their salt likes to talk about what they do and do not know. "Sure. We studied spear to strengthen our form and part of that training was defense against the spear."

"Good. The Valkyrja are priestesses of Odin, the bearer of the spear, Gungnir. You can expect that they will take a crack at skewering you."

Amber blinked slowly, took a deep breath, and then let it out in a controlled exhale. "So, this is serious, not a mock attack?"

I bobbed my head. "Very serious. You will probably fight twice, once against an unarmed opponent and once against one armed with a spear. The Sigrun will stop the fight if it looks like the priestess she has chosen to represent her is going to be bested or if you are clearly over-matched. Otherwise, she is going to wait to see who ends up unconscious or injured."

My pupil stared at me for a moment. "So, I have to go, pass the combat test, then what?"

I could not help smiling. "Then we get to the tough part. You meet the Sigrun and present your petition. Remember that her official title is Mother of Runes so you can address her as Mother or Sigrun. Do not act subservient in any way but be respectful - state what you want and why you want it plainly. The Sigrun has the final say but she will consult the Valkyrja present so you want to make a good impression on all of them. Once you have made your petition, you will be told to wait outside the Hall. When she has made her decision, you will be summoned. Be certain that you are where they left you, outside the Hall, no matter how long the decision takes."

Amber took this in then replied, "Where will you be?"

"I will be with you but I will not be allowed to speak or interfere in any way. It really is up to you."

Green eyes met mine. "What happens if the Sigrun decides in my favor?"

I shook my head. "I have no idea. I have never seen the Change accelerated before so I do not know what is involved. We are both on new ground there."

Amber huffed out a breath. Her scent had shifted subtly as we talked and I could smell the first tendrils of the acrid odor of fear.

I looked at her steadily again. "Are you sure you want to do this, Amber?"

My werewolf student gave a short laugh. "Hell, no, I don't want to do this! But I have been cast into a whole new world and, from what I can see, my best defense from the things that go bump in the night, things that I thought were not real or were just non-corporeal beings of folklore, is to become one of those things. The Sigrun cannot be much worse than my sifu on a bad day so let's do this thing. When do we leave?"

I smiled despite my own tension. I had vouched for Amber to the Sigrun and my reputation and standing in the Order were on the line. "We will leave at first light. No need to pack, I will be introducing you to a whole new way to get around tomorrow."

CHAPTER TEN

*T*he next morning, when Amber came down the stairs from her bedroom, I had to do a double take to be certain she was the same person I had seen trot up the steps. The ghost hunter had obviously showered and then tied her wet hair back in a thick braid. With the hair pulled back from her face, she looked more severe and that impression was not mitigated by her clothing. She had dressed in an all-black ensemble that looked like something a SEAL would wear into combat—black t-shirt of wicking material, black fatigue pants with enough pockets to store gear for a month and black mid-calf combat boots that would provide lots of ankle support and traction.

My pupil caught me staring and smiled. "A gift from my father's security detail. All ex-SAS anti-terrorism soldiers. They taught me how to shoot and some of the nastier points of unarmed combat."

Several remarks sprang into my head but all of them seemed inappropriate. Tactical gear never looked that good on me.

I moved my mind back to the business at hand, "We can take my trusty Xbox. We're just going over to the park."

* * *

THE PORTAL I wanted was in a copse of birch and maple in Delaware Park. As Amber and I walked across the field toward those trees, I murmured the Dawn rune, charging it with a little will so that those who might be watching would suddenly become interested in something else. Total invisibility is difficult to manage for even the most magically gifted beings. Distraction requires a much smaller power outlay and is much simpler to invoke.

I strode directly into the center of our tree cover with Amber close behind. I had explained to her that opening a Way required a good bit of concentration so she stood silently where I indicated as I took a deep breath, cleared my mind of everything but my purpose and set my will to the task of getting us into the Valkyrja's realm.

Not every magic that I do is runic. Black Dogs are supernatural creatures and we have innate magic of our own. Much of that magic is tied up with death and working with the dead but we are also one of many types of magical kin that can travel the Ways with relative ease.

Once I had opened my will, I extended my hand until I could 'feel' the intersection of several ley lines in the area like a hard nodule beneath my hand. I thrust both hands into that nodule, growling faintly in my chest as I accessed my power and parting my hands in a gesture that required more mental effort than physical. As I performed the first part of the opening, I focused on the line that would take us to the Valkyrja, visualizing the outer court of their temple, even as I turned my hands over and parted them vertically, opening the Way.

In the movies, when someone engages in interdimensional travel, there is usually an intense visual display with lots of lights and sound. In reality, if opening a Way made that much of a spectacle, few beings would risk using the Ways. The 'portal' that I had opened did not emit any light but instead appeared as a hazy rippling surface, like slightly disturbed pond water, in the shape of an arch.

I looked at Amber who was staring at the opening with some bemusement. "Expecting something more spectacular?" I asked.

She shook her head. "I wasn't sure what to expect honestly. There is still a part of me that is hoping this is just one of those really intense dreams and that I might wake up soon."

I gave her an appraising look. "Last chance. Are you sure you want to do this? It is not too late to head home and just wait for the moon."

Amber shook her head, the thick braid of her hair flopping over her shoulder. "Even if this is a dream, it has its own internal logic and part of that logic is that people are dying in the Adirondacks. I cannot walk away from that and choose to coddle myself. Let's go."

I extended my hand. "You will want to hold on to me. Get a good grip on my wrist and do not let go. I don't have time to teach you the finer points of running a Way so I am just going to haul you along with me."

The ghost hunter took a grip just shy of vice-like. I turned her toward the portal and strode into the opening without any further hesitation.

* * *

TRAVELING a Way is hard to describe. I've never skateboarded or surfed but I imagine, after watching humans do those things that the feeling of gliding along a Way is similar, only much, much faster. I heard Amber gasp and felt her grip tighten as we rocketed along the line that led to the Valkyrja temple but the trip was over before she could be afraid. Ordinarily, I would have simply stepped out of the Way onto solid ground but such an exit only comes with some practice. I had a very attractive but very solid female attached to my wrist in a death grip so I am afraid that our exit from the Way was less than graceful.

By the time we had picked ourselves up and dusted off our clothing, half a dozen spear carrying Valkyrja had us surrounded. I held my hands up cautiously, and slowly sketched the bind-rune that is given to each student who graduates from Valkyrja training. The symbol hung, glowing red in the air before me, and the warrior maidens relaxed slightly at the sight of it.

I felt Amber shiver behind me and upbraided myself for forgetting how cold it always was in the Valkyrja realms. Other than the involuntary reflex to the cold, my student simply stood her ground behind me and waited to see how the situation would unfurl. I noted, approvingly, that she had shifted into a comfortable, balanced stance from which she could move quickly in any direction. She might be cold but she was ready to fight.

One of the six Valkyrja, a blonde maiden with a wolf skin pelt pulled about her for warmth seemed to be in charge of their group. She looked to me and said, "State your business."

I stared at her and resisted the impulse to lock eyes and engage in the alpha contest. Such insolence was uncalled for; I had demonstrated that I was a member of the Order, although not, obviously, a full sister, and should have been treated with hospitality. My words came out brisk and clipped. "The Sigrun is expecting us. You would be wise not to keep her waiting, young pup." I gestured at the door of the massive wooden hall where I knew the Mother of Runes awaited us.

The Valkyrja did not take the insult well but the mention of the Sigrun brought her up short. She took her eyes from me for a moment—a distinct tactical error—and gestured with her head to a younger girl in the group, this one brunette but similarly attired in a piece of bear pelt. The younger maiden peeled away from the group and ran flat out for the door of the temple.

The young one was almost up the small flight of steps when the double doors of the hall opened and the Sigrun exited. The girl skidded to a halt in front of her superior and reported breathlessly even as the Sigrun made her way down the steps and into the courtyard to join us.

The Sigrun did not slow her stride until she stood next to the maiden who had challenged me. Without so much as a glimmer of intent, she hammered the girl into the ground with the haft of her spear and then, in a blinding flash, reversed the weapon, holding the gleaming point millimeters from the wide-eyed blonde's throat. "Child," she said in a voice low with threat, "when a being gives the sign of the Order, they are to be treated with hospitality, not arrogance. This one," she said, gesturing with her head at me, "could have ripped your throat out and left your body on the ground when you took your fool eyes off him. Do you understand?"

The girl nodded, afraid to speak. "Good," the Sigrun contin-ued, then addressed me, "is your companion prepared to meet her first challenge?"

I flicked a glance at Amber who had maintained her position even after the Sigrun's sudden movement. "I would say so, yes."

The Sigrun looked to me and the other Valkyrja with ice blue eyes. We stepped away from Amber and formed a loose circle. The Valkyrja butted their spears, no longer threatening but simply observing as Amber moved slowly into the center of the space, the hard-packed dirt puffing up around her boots. Once we had all moved out of the immediate combat area, the Sigrun reached down and ripped the spear from the hand of the young blonde before her and then gestured with her chin to the center of the circle.

Something I can only assume was pure excitement rose in the girl's eyes as she rose slowly and moved to face my pupil.

Hand to hand combat is never neat and choreographed. I had an instructor once who said that he never got a clean technique off in a real fight. As I watched Amber square off against the Valkyrja, I felt some real concern about this fight. I knew that my charge was skilled in Kung Fu but the Valkyrja were trained like special forces operators. Their technique was simple, direct, and lethal. I had no real idea how well Amber would handle a real-life attack with intent to cause serious damage. The ghost hunter's own scent told me that she was afraid but her training was serving her well. Her spine was straight, her stance strong, her body relaxed.

Amber bridged the gap between the two combatants in a blur, her fist extending in a right cross that would have done any boxer proud. The blonde went for the obvious attack and missed the slight rotation to her opponent's hip that was the bigger threat. Even as the Valkyrja moved into the cross and started into a throw, Amber's leading foot followed in a crescent kick that clipped the maiden cleanly in the jaw and put her down.

The Valkyrja rolled frantically to avoid the incoming stomp that would have finished the fight, shaking her head to try to clear the stars that were plainly swimming before her eyes. She scooped a handful of dirt from the ground and flung it full at Amber's face.

My pupil had obviously seen this tactic before and turned her head in time but she could not escape the forward charge of the blonde warrior, going down with her in a tangled heap. I held my breath. Valkyrja are trained to wrestle as well as strike and I knew that White Crane was not a ground fighting style.

For a moment, confusion reigned as the two women rolled on the ground, each seeking to take the upper position. The red earth smeared Amber's black garments as she struggled, avoiding the Valkyrja's attempt to get a hand on her throat. Just as she should have, Amber tucked her chin onto her chest to avoid the grasping hand and, while the blonde was intent on her purpose, threw an elbow that impacted solidly on the Valkyrja's floating ribs.

The blonde grunted with pain and Amber used the opportunity to try to shift her position upward. The Valkyrja was not having any of that and rolled clear of her red-headed opponent, coming to her feet as Amber rolled neatly away from her and sprang into a fighting crouch.

Something in the set of the Valkyrja's shoulders and the tightness of her expression signaled danger to me. I saw the Sigrun shift out of the corner of my eye; the Mother of Runes had seen something which alarmed her as well. Before either of us could cry foul, the blonde maiden pulled a wickedly sharp blade from her tunic and lunged at Amber in a straight, killing strike to the chest.

CHAPTER ELEVEN

*M*ost people, when confronted suddenly with a blade, flinch or shy away, trying to put distance between themselves and the cutting edge. This is rarely a successful tactic and often results in a cut or worse. My student, though, moved into the strike, shifting her body at the last possible instant and sustaining a deep but superficial cut across her shoulder. I heard the hiss of pain as the blade sliced her but her face showed nothing but grim resolve as she moved inside her opponent's attack and threw an elbow that cleanly broke the blonde's collarbone.

The Valkyrja screamed in agony as Amber hammered down on the break. The knife slipped from nerveless hands as my pupil slammed her opponent into the packed earth and flipped her neatly onto her stomach. As the blonde writhed in pain, Amber placed both hands under the maiden's chin, pulling her back until it was plain that she could snap the Valkyrja's back if she chose. Her sides heaving, Amber looked to the Sigrun for direction, just as I had told her. The Sigrun seemed to contemplate for a moment and I could see the terror in the blonde maiden's eyes, sure that her death was about to find her. After a moment of contemplation, the Mother of Runes looked at Amber and said, "Please release her, warrior."

Amber leaned down and said something into the blonde's ear. My ears were sharp enough to pick up what she said. "Next time, perhaps you will have more respect. I am going to let you go. If you try anything, I will make sure that you never see combat again. Clear?"

The blonde attempted to nod and Amber released her slowly, getting well clear of the warrior before relaxing her guard slightly. My student moved into the center of the circle again as two of the maidens, at a silent signal from the Sigrun, picked up their comrade and hauled her off toward the gates of the courtyard. The Valkyrja had disgraced her Order; the Sigrun had not given permission for her to use weapons nor had she given any indication that she wished Amber dead. Such a breach of discipline could only have one result.

The Valkyrja, wounded and disgraced, would be taken to the healer outside the gates to have her injuries attended and, once that had been accomplished, would be thrown into a cell to await the Sigrun's judgment. There was little doubt in my mind that the young woman would be stripped of any magics she might have acquired and deposited unceremoniously outside the gates. If she attempted to return, she would be killed summarily.

I shrugged. "As I told you, Mother, this one is full of surprises."

The Sigrun eyed Amber standing quietly in the center of the circle, obviously curious to see what would happen next, but holding her peace. "Yes, she is . . . what was the word you used? Exceptional?"

Amber darted a quick look at me and then returned her attention to the Mother of Runes. The Sigrun returned her regard with an openly curious gaze. "You did not tell me that this one Belonged to one of the great goddesses."

"She does have the Oracle's sense, Mother, but she is untrained. I am sorry that I did not think to mention it," I replied.

The Sigrun turned her attention to my charge. "How are you called, child?"

"Amber, Mother." I was interested to note that she did not give her full name but then I realized that, in all the lore books that she had obviously consumed, she was bound to have run across the idea that the true name of anything gives you power over it.

The Sigrun laughed again, peering closely at the dirt smeared woman. "You need not fear that I will seek power over you, child, but it is well that you exercise caution. Amber is a good name. In natural magic, amber is used as a protective device. It hardens the aura and makes it much more difficult to psychically attack the wearer."

The older woman eyed Amber and seemed to come to a decision. "I've already spoken to the Black Dog about your situation. I have seen you fight and I have seen you with eyes other than those I have in my old head. Ordinarily, I would require more testing but I understand that the situation is dire, that the Beast hunts your area of the Midlands and must be stopped. I believe that you can come through the Change with your sanity intact so I am willing to do as you and the Black Dog have requested, on one condition."

Amber looked at the old priestess and said quietly, "Name your condition, Mother, I am listening."

"Once this hunt is done, you must return and take the training that you need to be a full Oracle. We are priestesses of Odin and we know the old ways of that training. We can teach you to hear the voice of your Lady more clearly. Hekate is an old family friend, in a manner of speaking."

Amber's eyes practically glowed as she answered, "Mother, I would be deeply honored to learn anything that you and your Order will teach me."

The Sigrun clapped her hands and the remaining Valkyrja dispersed almost instantly. "It is settled then. We will do the working once the moon is up tonight. In the meantime, you must come into the hall, have that wound attended, feast and then rest. It will be a long night for all of us."

* * *

WHEN THE SIGRUN of the Valkyrja tells you that you're going to feast, she isn't jesting. Amber and I sat at the long trestle tables in the hall and were served course after course until neither of us was capable of eating another bite. The Sigrun, recalling my eating habits, even supplied me with a piece of linen to tie around my neck so that my clothes would not get bloodstained. It felt almost natural to sit at the table, my face partly shifted, wolfing down chunks of delectable lamb, as my meal companion ate with equal relish on the other side of the table. The Sigrun did not eat as she was going to be working high magic that night but she kept us company as we laid waste to the Valkyrja larder.

At length though, even a new werewolf and a hungry Black Dog will eat their fill. The Sigrun chuckled as we practically rolled ourselves away from the table. "It is good to see that you are still in good appetite, Black Dog. I kept our hunters busy feeding you when you were here. You know where the guest quarters are—I suggest that you two avail yourselves of them."

I hesitated for a moment. The guest quarters were a single room with a single, albeit large, bed. The Valkyrja did not get a lot of visitors and those that came normally came alone. I let Amber know about this as we made our way up the hand-carved wooden stairway, with its insets of tales from the myths of Odin, and she just looked at me. "Zach," she said, rolling her eyes, "you've been a perfect gentleman over the past few days, even when you might have taken advantage of my vulnerability. I have absolutely no problem with sharing a bed with you. Or, are you uncomfortable for another reason?"

I shook my head but my mouth started talking before my brain could override. "I have not spent this much time in the presence of an attractive woman in a long time. I would be lying if I said that I had not had . . . thoughts."

To my surprise, the beautiful redhead reached over and stroked my chin, much as she had when she had first seen me shifted to eat. "And I have not spent much time in the presence of a man who was not after my money, or just looking for a fling. You are not the only one having thoughts, Zachary Collins, but I need some time to adjust to what is ahead of me before I give that too much consideration."

I nodded, not trusting myself to speak, then closed the gap between us and kissed her full lips lightly. "I agree." I murmured, "We have to survive the next few days."

Her eyes were heavy-lidded as they looked up at me and I could smell a very welcome shift in her scent. "Do that again, and I might throw caution to the wind."

I put my hand on the side of her face and she held it to her warm cheek. "I am not going to," I said, "not because I don't want to but because I don't want to be a selfish bastard. You are going to need every ounce of energy you possess tonight. You need to be sleeping, not engaged in other activities."

Amber smiled up at me. "I was wrong."

"About what?" I asked, hoping I had not offended her.

"I thought that Allan Greenwood was the knightly sort. I think you have him beat."

I had to laugh at that. "Nah, I have just been around long enough to have a little more control of my urges than a human who looks my age."

Amber backed away from me a step. "I keep forgetting the whole magical creature thing. How old are you exactly?"

I took a deep breath. "I was born in December of 1792."

My student's eyes widened slightly but then she stepped back into me and put her arms around me. "I always did have a thing for older men."

Before I could carry that thought further, I took her hand and led her up to the guest quarters, helped her out of her boots and then tucked her firmly into the bed. Once she was settled. I snatched up a bearskin lying at the foot of the bed and pulled it over me, using my training to force myself down to sleep before I could think about the not altogether unpleasant rush of hormones moving through my system.

CHAPTER TWELVE

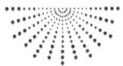

I woke two hours later with Amber curled up against my side, her head resting lightly in the crook of my shoulder. I tried to extricate myself from the warm nest we had made in our sleep without waking her but, as soon as I moved, her eyes popped open. I rolled quickly to my side of the bed and threw my legs over the edge. A knock sounded on the door and I called, "Enter!"

The dark-haired Valkyrja who had witnessed the fight that afternoon stuck her head in the door. "The Sigrun bids you come."

I thanked the girl and told her that we would be down in a few moments. Amber had replaced her boots by the time I turned back to her and looked at me with quirked brows. "What?" I asked, curious about her expression.

"I'd have thought that you woke up next to a rattlesnake, the way you came out of bed."

I smiled, "That is because your senses have not undergone the full transformation yet. I could hear the young lady coming down the hall."

"And you did not want the Sigrun thinking that we were . . . doing something other than sleeping?"

"The Sigrun would have been most, shall we say, disappointed in me had I not allowed you to rest. I strive to avoid that disappointment—a lesson I learned with many bruises and cuts when I trained here."

Amber looked concerned. "Crap! Am I going to have to scrap it on with some gung-ho shield maiden every time I come here?"

I grinned and shook my head. "No, you have proven yourself a warrior and a damn good one too, I might add. Most people could not have avoided that knife today."

Amber shrugged. "I told you that my father's security detail taught me the nastier points of unarmed combat. Knife defense was one of those things. And I can shoot an eye out with a 9-millimeter at twenty-five-yards."

I whistled under my breath. "Well, you do not have to worry about proving yourself again. You have shown that you have a warrior's spirit. The training of an Oracle is much gentler and more centered on meditation and guidance than my training was. You might equate my training with the Valkyrja as the magical equivalent of what you learned from your SAS contingent."

Amber looked me up and down with something approaching respect. "So, you magically got your ass kicked on a regular basis so that you could learn how to avoid getting it kicked?"

I laughed. "That about sizes it up. Now, let's go. The Sigrun does not wait well."

Amber moved out the door with alacrity. Apparently, my old teacher had made an impression on her. I followed, closing the door as we went and following the ghost hunter down the stairs and into the main hall.

The Sigrun awaited us, seated in the high seat at the front of the room. Without a word, she rose and met us halfway across the room, leading us silently out the massive double doors that led into the courtyard. Without any seeming effort, the Mother of Runes made a complex sign in the space before her and a flaming red Ing rune appeared before her, expanded, and formed a portal. The old priestess stepped forward, through the Gate, and gestured for us to follow.

* * *

ONCE I HAD OVERCOME the slight disorientation of the transition from one place to another on the Other Side, I looked around to find our party in a clearing in the midst of a dense oak forest. Evening had been falling at the Great Hall but, in this place, full dark had descended, the darkness an almost palpable presence as I got my bearings. In the center of the grove was the stump of a lightning damaged tree and torches had been hung at intervals from the branches to provide some light for the working. At a Word from the Sigrun, the torches sprang to light, bathing the clearing in flickering light and leaving Amber slightly wide-eyed.

The Mother of Runes gave Amber a moment to orient herself and then spoke softly. "To the west, you will find a short trail. Follow that trail to a smaller clearing where you will find a chest bound with metal straps. Bring me the contents of that chest, child, while I make some other preparations."

Amber nodded and departed without a word. Apparently, she had decided that asking questions was only going to delay the inevitable. I looked to the Sigrun and she spoke to me, sub-vocally so that only I could hear. "She is strong but you understand what you must do if she loses control?"

I nodded wondering why she would ask such a thing of a Black Dog. Seeming to read my thoughts, the Sigrun continued, "I can see that there is something more than friendship in your heart, Black Dog. It is not fully formed or consummated but I need to know that your feelings for the woman will not impede your duty, should it come to that."

Damn! Had I been so transparent or was it simply the Mother

of Runes' powers of observation that led to this conversation. I pulled myself up straight and lifted my chin. "I am not old, as Black Dogs go, Mother, but I know my duty and I am sworn to it. If things go awry, I will do what must be done."

The Sigrun gazed at me, her face intent in the moving light. After a long moment, she nodded. "Good. Go and Change then. I will key the circle to admit you but stay outside unless you are needed." She pulled a twine wrapped package from beneath her cloak and set it on the ground next to her.

I nodded and slipped away into the dark forest. After draping my clothes over a tree branch, I dropped, naked and on all fours, to the ground and reached deep within, turning my form inside out to reveal my True Self. I stretched, popping loose the tension of the day, and, shaking my fur into place, I trotted back toward the grove.

I settled silently in the deep shadow of a great oak just outside the perimeter of the clearing. I turned my head, checking to make sure I had a clear view of the proceedings and raising my nose to the wind to be certain that I would be able to detect any dangerous changes in Amber's scent. I allowed my eyes to flare, lighting my locations with a hellish red, so that the Sigrun would know I was on station and ready.

My dog mind sat at the forefront, aware only of its duty and what must be done if the werewolf went rogue, but the more human part of me was silently praying that all would go well. I did not want to Hunt this woman. Something startling occurred to my human mind. The Dog did not want to hunt the werewolf either. It wanted to make her a part of its pack.

I did not have time to chew on this revelation. Amber strode quietly back into the clearing and handed the Sigrun a long strip of wolf fur. The Mother of Runes whispered something to the soon to be werewolf and I could see color leap to Amber's cheeks. She scooped up the package on the ground and walked a short distance into the wood. I could tell but the scraping of her belt buckle, the rustle of cloth and the release of her scent that she had removed her clothes. She emerged, hesitantly, into the clearing, with a long woolen cloak pulled tightly around her.

The Sigrun smiled, almost gently, at her. "If you are to be a wolf, child, you will have to get used to being unclothed. There must never be anything on your body that would restrict the Change when you choose to make It. All clothing and most jewelry must come off or the magic will not work."

Amber nodded. "I understand, Mother. I don't know enough about magic to really have an idea what to expect."

The Sigrun nodded. "We will teach you. For now, the Black Dog has taught you the rules of the Charter which govern your kind. Because you have asked it of me, and because you have accepted the condition that I laid earlier, I am going to help you make a Change outside the tide of the Moon. I would ask you once more if you wanted to go forward but I can see determination in your eyes. So, let us begin. I want you to seat yourself comfortably at the base of this stump and calm yourself as much as you can."

Amber nodded, her face tight with anticipation. Even the Dog noted how beautiful she looked, her flame red hair spilling over the dark cloak, the torchlight glowing warm along the side of her face. She settled in the indicated spot and moved the folds of the cloak so that they covered most of her bare skin. In my fur form, I really did not notice the cool of the descending night but I was certain that bare human flesh would feel it.

As I watched, the ghost hunter closed her eyes and took three deep breaths, moving the air into the depths of her belly and breathing it all out again. Once she had taken the cleansing breaths, she allowed her inhalations and exhalations to settle into a deep regular rhythm. Her shoulders dropped as she invoked the relaxation response and her body settled, almost seeming to become a part of the stump against which she was propped.

"Good," the Sigrun said, softly so as not to startle, "you have had some training in meditation. That is useful. I am going to walk around the perimeter of this grove. As I do that, I want you to begin imagining, in your mind's eye, a wolf. Not just any wolf, Amber, but your wolf. I want you to see the wolf that you will become. See it clearly. Can you do that?"

Amber nodded, half in trance from her deep relaxation. "Yes, Mother."

CHAPTER THIRTEEN

*A*s Amber sought within for her inner wolf, the Mother of Runes prepared the space in which she would work.

The Sigrun rose slowly and moved to the northern edge of the grove. Calmly and clearly, she traced the Elk rune, invoking the protection of Asgard upon the place of her working. She gazed at the flaming rune, etched in sylvan light before her, and held her arms out to the side at a 45-degree angle to mimic the rune. She murmured the Name of the rune over and over in that stance until the symbol shone with scintillating fire across the northern quarter of the clearing.

When she was satisfied, the old priestess reached into the heart of the coruscating energy and, seeming to grab a handful, pulled the light to the east where she repeated her invocation and raising of energy, moving then to the south and then to the west before closing the circle again at the north and returning to the center where Amber sat, concentrating hard on her appointed task. Facing north, the Sigrun raised her hands in the Elk posture once more and traced the rune above and below to complete a Sphere of Protection that not even a Faery Lord could breach.

I stood, admiring my teacher's handiwork, and feeling the

subtle shift in the field as I prowled closer to check it out. Yes, it would yield to me if the time came for me to enter, but for now, Amber and the Sigrun were safe inside.

In the high magic tradition of her Order, the Sigrun now had to hallow the stead. For most, this would have been a major Summoning but, for the leader of the Valkyrja, her god was as close as a few spoken words of the Havamal.

The trees around me shifted as though moved by a silent wind and a whispering voice, whiskey dark and deadly, but, at the same time, filled with the promise of caress, answered my teacher's call. The air was filled with the smell of old blood, long shed and dried, strong liquor, rum perhaps, and most oddly, cigars. I could not see the Sigrun's face, deep in the folds of her hood, but the set of her body and the scent of her flesh reminded me of a woman greeting a lover that she had not seen in some time.

Whispered words of greeting were exchanged in a voice so low even I could not hear. To my surprise, the Sigrun began another chant. This time there was no softness to the invocation; her voice cut clearly across the grove, ringing out into the wild-wood but, more importantly, sounding a bell on the astral plane, the words in a form of Greek that had not been used in the Midlands in a thousand years.

Again, the fur of my hackles rose as another of the Powers came to share this space. I nearly sneezed as the air was filled with the smell of dust, dry and moldy; a rare and aged musk, delicate and sweet with dark undertones that pulled the mind toward the shadows, and the salt tang of the sea.

Amber started from meditation at the touch of her goddess but the Sigrun gestured her back to trance. The Mother of Runes spoke swiftly; liquid syllables poured from her lips and, though I could not understand the speech, I gathered the context. The Sigrun was explaining to Amber's patroness what we proposed to do and why. She was seeking the permission of the Lady to whom Amber Belonged before proceeding. A voice like a hundred whispers sewn together with cobwebs replied after several moments and the Sigrun bowed low speaking a word of thanks and giving what sounded like a license to depart.

Harsh laughter filled the air and the Presence in the West stayed right where it was. Whatever happened, Hekate intended to stay. The chief priestess of the Valkyrja seemed to give a mental shrug and then turned to her charge in the center of the circle.

The Sigrun walked slowly over to Amber and knelt next to her. "Tell me about your wolf, Amber."

The ghost hunter dropped the hood of the cloak back, her red hair shining in the torchlight, and looked to the Sigrun. "I felt . . . Hekate?"

The priestess smiled, "Yes, She is here with you but I need you to concentrate on the task at hand. Tell me about your wolf."

Amber's eyes stared off into the middle distance as she spoke, "The wolf that I see is long and lean. Not bulky and powerful like some of the timber wolves I have seen, more like the wolves of the desert, long-legged and built for endurance, I guess. Her pelt is grey but has strong red highlights. Her eyes are gold."

The Sigrun looked off into the middle distance with her and then turned to Amber and said. "Good. That is the wolf that I see as well. Now, can you see yourself as this wolf? Does it feel real to you? How does your body feel?"

Amber shook herself slightly as though fighting sleep and I realized that, even though the Sigrun was speaking to her, the old priestess was also bringing her power to bear, taking Amber into a semi-trance state. At last, Amber said, "I feel odd, Mother. My skin feels tingly and . . . strange. As though it does not fit quite right. There is a horrible itching at the base of my spine and my face feels like something is pulling on it."

The Sigrun stroked Amber's brow lightly and I sensed the thin veil of magic that dropped over the ghost hunter as the

Mother of Runes worked her spell of transformation. "Good, child. I want you to picture that wolf you saw earlier. Picture it in your mind as clearly as you can."

Amber's hand clenched the forearm of the priestess. "I see it. It is walking toward me."

"Yes. It will come toward you and then it will walk into you."

A shudder ran through the body of the un-Changed werewolf and her face took on a distinctly vulpine cast, her eyes turning gold and her body bending forward as she gasped in an involuntary breath.

The Sigrun ran her hand over Amber's brow once more and bade her be calm. The lovely redhead took a shaky breath and the exhalation came out as a growl. She started back and the Sigrun grabbed both hands in an iron grip. "Do not fight, child, you will only make the Change harder. Focus on the wolf."

Amber whined deeply then managed to find her human voice, although it came out lower and rougher than normal. "I am afraid, Mother. I feel the animal trying to take over completely and it hungers. I do not want to hurt you."

The Sigrun gazed into her face and laughed softly, "This is not the first time I have done this, child, I have defenses should you lose control but you will not." The last words were uttered with power and Amber seemed to relax a little.

As she stopped fighting, the magic of the Sigrun gained the upper hand. Amber's jaw began to extend, much as mine did when I shifted for feeding and I could see her hands curling into themselves, becoming paws even as I watched. The ghost hunter pitched forward onto the ground, laying, panting, on her side as the Change accelerated.

The Sigrun draped the cloak modestly over Amber's Changing form and began a soft chant. The old priestess was calling to the human inside Amber, calling to bring her forward even as the werewolf's body heaved and rippled, a stunted cry of pain escaping lips that were rapidly receding to be replaced by powerful jaws and a keen black nose.

I flinched inwardly at the deep crack of bone and sinew unbinding and then re-knitting itself into a new form. The Change was progressing so rapidly that I was unsure if the Sigrun would be able to call Amber's mind to the fore and give her control. I stalked close to the edge of the circle and called upon the fire in my soul, bringing power to the magic innate in my kind. Death walked at my shoulder as I came to do the duty required of Black Dogs from time immemorial.

Inside the circle, the Sigrun had wisely moved away from the rapidly Changing wolf. The priestess of Odin continued her chant, striving to call forth that which was the human, Amber Morgan, within the gray wolf with red highlights in its pelt that was trying to rise to its feet.

The new wolf rose slowly and shook off the cloak, its nostrils flaring, ears rotating through several directions, eyes staring in an effort to focus as it became accustomed to the new level of sensory input. I could see confusion in its eyes but no sign of Amber as its head swiveled and homed on the scent of the Sigrun, standing in the west.

CHAPTER FOURTEEN

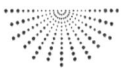

$\mathcal{T}$he Sigrun never stopped her chant, only increased its volume and cadence even as she kept her distance from the long- legged canid in the circle.

The wolf stopped and flicked its ears, shaking its head as though trying to clear away a buzzing fly. It took another step but set its foot down wrong and swerved to the side drunkenly. The animal growled low and continued to stare as the Sigrun ignored it, lost in her chant and seemingly unaware of the danger.

I knew better, the Sigrun carried her spear and knew how to use it, but I would not take chances with my master's life. I stepped carefully through the edge of the circle, feeling the stinging ant sensation along my flesh as I breached the magical barrier and crept up behind the wolf.

There was no hint of a breeze inside the circle but some instinct in the wolf made it glance back over its shoulder to see me. The wolf that had been Amber turned slowly to face me, its head lowered and a growl slipping through the snarling fangs. A careful assessment of the wolf's body language showed me that this was fear aggression but it was aggression nonetheless and my Dog would not abide such behavior in a werewolf. I dropped my own head, pricked my hackles, and growled low, the vibration emanating from deep in my chest. I could tell from the red glare in front of me that my eyes had flared in response to the danger.

The wolf backed away slowly, ears against the sides of its head, fangs showing, but the tail was tucked. This one would not fight unless forced to and my human part was trying to give the Sigrun enough time to call Amber through to her wolf. I moved sideways, keeping my eye on the wolf and herding it away from the priestess.

Once more, the red pelted canid stopped and shook its head. I wondered if the Sigrun's charm was having an effect but then the wolf surprised me. Rather than going for the first available kill, the wolf sought to escape by running full tilt away from me toward the dark forest which surrounded us both.

Of course, the wolf galloped full steam into the enchanted barrier and knocked itself down. As it lay stunned for a moment, I moved to cover the Sigrun, still standing in the west. Amber's wolf had gotten the hang of its new body and was now even more dangerous.

The wolf recovered from its encounter with magical protections quickly and came to its feet again. It stalked back and forth, eyeing the Sigrun and I but seemingly unable to decide how to proceed. Physics sometimes does not apply to werewolves but Amber had transformed into a wolf that weighed almost exactly what she did in human form. My True Self, on the other hand, is a massive hound that outweighed the female wolf by over a hundred pounds. The wolf was starved, after its Change, but its instinct told it that there was no way it was going to get through me for a meal or make a meal out of me. There was also no way for it to escape this space so that it could find food, human or otherwise, elsewhere. Desperation was slowly seeping into the wolf's eyes and that made it even more dangerous. I could not play this game with Amber's wolf forever. Eventually, she was going to do something that was going to make me put her down unless the Sigrun could succeed in getting through to her.

The end came sooner than I had imagined. At the end of one of its long swings across the opposite end of the magical "cage", the wolf broke off and darted for the Sigrun.

I am a Black Dog. One of the things that most werewolves don't realize about my kind is that, despite our mass, we are preternaturally fast. Amber's wolf found this out the hard way when I slammed my shoulder into her, knocking her from her feet before she was even halfway to the priestess. She managed to curl in on herself and come to her feet neatly but, before the final Hunt could begin, several things happened within the space of a couple of seconds.

As the wolf made her charge, the Sigrun had lowered her spear and pointed it at the animal. I thought that she was preparing to defend herself but, as I knocked the wolf out of play, she pointed the glittering tip of the blade at the creature and unleashed a stream of flowing syllables in the ancient Greek that she had been speaking before.

It dawned on me that the Sigrun had chosen her position purposely as Power gathered behind her. The tip of the spear glowed with that Power as the priestess of Odin once more evoked the Power of her god's distant relative. The scent of dust and musk and seawater flooded the circle and the ground seemed to undulate under my paws as the cobwebbed voice I had heard earlier spoke a name—Amber Katarina Morgan.

The wolf stopped, frozen in place by the Power of the Word and then dropped to the ground on its stomach, its face abject and confused, as one mind struggled with the other for supremacy. I knew we had won when the wolf's eyes turned brilliant green for a moment, then shaded slowly back to gold. I looked into those eyes and saw intelligence there, intelligence and remorse.

I kept my distance, just in case, but lowered my head slightly as I spoke, mind to mind, softly as I could, "Amber?"

The wolf's ears pricked and her tongue fell from her mouth in a lolling grin, "Oh my . . . Zach?"

I moved my head in affirmation. "I thought we'd lost you for a minute," I remarked.

The golden eyed wolf huffed and moved a step forward, its ears flat and eyes wide. "I was trying to get through but the Change happened so quickly that I got, I don't know, stuck behind the wolf."

The Sigrun stepped up beside me, spear at the ready. "Is all well, Black Dog?"

In response, I moved over to Amber and licked her muzzle.

The Sigrun nodded thoughtfully and spoke words of thanks to both of the Powers present before unwinding the circle. Amber and I waited quietly as the wards came down and the Sigrun snuffed the torches with a wave of her hand.

Once my master had grounded all the energies, she re-opened the portal and turned to us. "Well, my children, a good night's work but this old woman is done in. I am going to rest for a few hours but I will be back for you by the time the sun rises in this place. Go, Amber, child of Hekate, and acquaint yourself with this new form."

Without looking back, the Sigrun stepped through the portal and closed it behind her. I looked over at Amber and could see excitement lighting her eyes. "So, what would you like to do first, o' new wolf?"

Amber did not hesitate. "I think you better teach me something about hunting. I'm starved."

With that, she was off into the woods like a shot, a huge Black Dog at her heels.

* * *

WE SPENT the night bounding through the forest, feasting on small game, and playing hide and seek to get Amber used to her wolf form. It was important that she learn stealth so I showed her how to judge the wind and where it was coming from, how to shrink down into the shadows to hide, how to use the cover of the wood to break up the outline of her form and make her less visible. We drilled over and over until she managed to evade me for half an hour and then we worked on tracking until I was confident that she could and would use her nose in addition to her other senses.

In between lessons, I took her back to the clearing and made her Change twice more, coaching her and watching her carefully to be certain that she had the knack of calling her human mind into the wolf form.

Eventually, between the lessons and the Changes, the werewolf and I flopped down in the clearing where the Sigrun would come for us and dozed off, exhausted by the night's work. I woke shortly before dawn, keenly aware of the warm fur and lean muscle of Amber's wolf curled against my back but shook my thoughts clear and got Amber up so that we could be prepared for the Sigrun's arrival.

As I EXPECTED, the Mother of Runes came for Amber and I shortly after dawn, materializing from a Portal but not closing it behind her, the surface of the gate rippling the space behind her. The expression on her face, the slight tension in her shoulders and the whiteness of the knuckles gripping her spear told me that she brought bad tidings. "What is it, Mother?"

If Amber had been in wolf form, her ears would have perked up. I noted, with approval, that she was studying the Sigrun' stance, trying to understand what had told me that something was wrong. The Sigrun saw it too and her blue eyes sparkled with wry humor for just a moment before her lips tightened. "The elf contacted me last night when I arrived back at the hall. He says to tell you that there has been another confirmed kill in your territory and that the assistance that you requested was available."

My gut clenched at the news and the color drained from Amber's face. I had hoped to have a couple more days with the new werewolf to help her be more prepared but the Beast was forcing my hand. "It was an open kill, Mother?"

The old priestess moved her head slightly. "Worse than that, it was an open challenge. The Beast killed one of Greenwood's employees, a young woman who had been researching for him. I tell you, Black Dog, that I have never seen the elf so angry; he was ready to Hunt this rogue himself. You know how he is about those under his protection."

The Mother of Runes continued before I could speak. "I finally persuaded him that, though he has formidable skills, he should leave the werewolf hunting to the kindred that have been doing it for thousands of years. He agreed, reluctantly, but he is not happy. There will be blood if this young lady is not avenged; I believe that he will call a Hunt, if you are not successful."

I looked grimly at the runemaster, struggling for something to say as Amber moved up beside me and took my arm gently. The Sigrun turned toward the portal back to the hall and gestured for us to follow as she stepped through, back to her home. Moving more like a zombie than a Black Dog, I stepped automatically into the Way, half dragging Amber with me.

The new werewolf said nothing as we arrived in the dusty courtyard where, not long before, Amber had bested one of the Sigrun's Valkyrja. I was ready to make the jump back into the Midlands but the Sigrun stopped me with a motion of her hand. "Come inside, child, have something to eat. I have a something that I wish to give you before you go."

CHAPTER FIFTEEN

I bridled at any delay for a moment but then realized that, after the night's exertions, I was still hungry. Only the gods knew when I might get a chance to eat again and one did not turn down an "invitation" from the Mother of Runes. I nodded and Odin's priestess led the way into the hall, seating us at the trestle table once more and signaling to the attending Valkyrja apprentices for sustenance to be brought.

While we waited for the food to appear, the Sigrun walked over behind the high seat where she normally presided and returned with a small wooden cask that bore a silver plate atop it etched with runes. Looking at the symbols on the plate, I realized that the box was keyed so that anyone opening it, besides the Sigrun, would be in for a very nasty death by lightning strike.

The Mother of Runes produced a key on a silver chain from beneath her robe and opened the casket, drawing out an item wrapped in silk and placing it on the table before me.

The Sigrun regarded me carefully for a moment and then moved back around the table to me. She unwrapped the silk of the package before me and I gasped. I knew what it was but I could not believe that it was being presented to me.

The Sigrun smiled, her blue eyes bright in her wrinkled face. "Did you think that we had been ignoring your progress, Zachary? The Valkyrja train beings to be magical warriors. We train you to fight hand to hand and we train you to combat magic with magic. We have followed your career amongst your kindred for years and you have never failed to distinguish yourself amongst your peers. You took the training that we gave you, training in how to be adaptable and move with the flow of a combat, and you have used it, bringing in dozens, if not hundreds of rogue wolves, sometimes without ever striking a blow or casting a spell. Now, you have been given your own territory and you face a terrible threat. Granting you your staff is the least we could do to assist you."

I stared down at the silver headpiece that the Sigrun had unwrapped, momentarily at a loss for words. This piece was obviously wrought by human hands but the craftsmanship was magnificent. It was a Bind-rune skillfully wrought to contain all twenty-four runes of the Elder Futhark. As I sat contemplating the piece, the Sigrun produced a six feet length of ash from beneath the table and handed it over to me.

I confess that my hands shook as I placed the headpiece atop the staff. I looked to the Sigrun and she nodded permission. Slowly and carefully, I spoke the motto of the Valkyrja in the Old Norse:

Chooser of the Slain, am I
Rider of the Grey Horse,
Eight-legged Sleipnir
The worlds unfold beneath me
Odhinn walks with me
Wisdom be my guide
Magic be my tool
Battle be my life.

As I FINISHED the short phrase, I felt power rise from the earth through the staff, the power of Hel, the realm of the dead, cold and red and fierce like the glowing of my eyes in battle, while, at the same time, the powers of Asgard flowed from above, striking the headpiece and giving off a brilliant flare of light that forced everyone in the room to turn their eyes away for a moment. I still had my hand on the staff, though practically blind, and I felt the powers winding together, interlocking and smelled the ash burning beneath my grip.

When I could see again, the headpiece was welded firmly to the ash staff and runes had burned themselves in a winding pattern down the length of the wood, still smoking as I caressed the smooth stick.

The Sigrun drew herself up formally, "It seems that the staff has accepted you," she commented dryly, bringing a couple of muffled chuckles from the young retainers coming into the hall to feed us, "ordinarily, there would be a feast in your honor but we know that you have urgent business to attend. Use the staff well, Zachary Collins, Black Dog, adept of the Order of the Valkyrja and return to us so that we may honor you as is fit."

* * *

AMBER and I stepped back through the node where we had departed, what seemed like days before, and spent a couple of moments in the copse of birch and maple, re-orienting ourselves to the Midlands and where we were on the face of the planet. I spent a little time guiding Amber through the process of grounding so that we both felt better when we slipped from the trees and made our way back to the Xbox. I admit I felt both self-conscious and better protected as the heavy wooden staff thunked the sidewalk in time with my stride.

I had barely gotten buckled into the driver's seat when my phone rang. I knew who it was without looking and punched the button to answer the device.

"You heard?" the voice on the line said without preamble.

"The Sigrun told me when she came to get Amber and me." "This rogue of yours has made it personal now. Kyla Tedesco wasn't just an employee; she was a friend."

"You know that I will not let this animal go free, Al-lin. Send everything you have to my GRI account." "Then what?"

"Then," I said, my mouth tight and my breathing controlled to keep my eyes from flaring, "then I go hunting."

Greenwood grunted assent on the end of the line. "Your trip was a success then? The girl is somewhat ready to accompany you?"

I nodded, glancing at Amber who, with her newly acute ears, could hear every word of the conversation. "It was very success-ful. We had some problems getting the human to come through on the first Change. A close call but we had some . . . divine inter-vention to assist us. She is in good shape now and changes faster than any wolf I have ever seen."

"Good. I'm glad this mess did not take any more lives. I am having Kevin send you all the latest information that we have," Al-lin paused and I sensed what was coming, "including complete forensics from the last victim. I had one of our contract people in to look at the body. There is no doubt that she was attacked by a werewolf."

Amber raised an eyebrow and I motioned to her that I would explain later. She nodded and settled back into her seat. "The Sigrun says that I am going up against the Beast, Al-lin. They even awarded me my staff while I was there."

I could almost see Al-lin's long face breaking into a pained smile. "The Sigrun seems to have a talent for awarding those things when the recipient is about to go into a killing field, Black Dog. The Old One must think you are in for a fight if she parted with it. If you will recall, I got mine when I went up against Edward Blacklake."

That story was, of course, legendary amongst the supernatural community of Buffalo. One of the Guild Warriors had been dispatched to bring in an untrained wizard of enormous potential, Tamara Jenkins. The young warrior, Johann Mayer, successfully brought in the lady, and subsequently ended up married to her, but only after Jenkins sucker punched Edward Blacklake, the local Duke of the Unseelie Court, during an attempt on her life that almost cost her lover his own.

Blacklake, who should have simply acknowledged the loss and gone on, became obsessed with revenge, making several attempts on Jenkin's life over the course of the next year. Since he was in violation of the Charter, both the Guild Warriors and the Justiciars of the Faery were looking for Blacklake but no one could find him until Al-lin became involved.

One of Al-lin's employees had gotten caught in the crossfire during the last attempt on Tamara Jenkin's life. Al-lin had invoked one of the oldest magics of Faery, the blood link between Sidhe of both courts, and forced Blacklake to trial by combat. It is said that the field where the two met for the duel was now one of the only places in Faery where nothing would grow. The Sigrun had granted Al-lin his staff just before the ordeal began.

"I do recall that, yes. I am hoping that I will not have to lay waste to a whole mountain in order to get this rogue."

Amber's eyebrow shot up again and I saw her look with interest at the staff in the rear section of the car. Al-lin replied smoothly, "I hope so too. This contest will happen in the Midlands and will be much harder to hide than the contest between Edward and myself. I know that you said you wanted certain assets within a thirty- minute helicopter ride of your position. I have taken the liberty of getting them a little closer. We've established a base camp at a private airstrip just south of the High Peaks Wilderness. Response time to any location in that area should be no more than fifteen minutes. They will be armed to stop anything up to and including a tank."

Amber looked at me with mouth open and I mouthed "SAS" to her. She nodded. "I am glad to hear that," I replied, "and I presume that you will be on the scene as well?"

"I am leaving by helicopter once Edward has assured me that you have everything we have."

I nodded, thinking fast. "That is even better. I hope that I do not have to call your team in."

I could hear Al-lin nod. "I hope so, too. Good hunting, Black Dog."

CHAPTER SIXTEEN

I dropped Amber off at her house so that she could get cleaned up and pack while I went back to my lair and did the same. Technically, I should not have left Amber alone, even though she had demonstrated good control over her Change, but even I cannot be two places at one time and I did not want to waste time I could spend hunting.

Black Dog Academy training drives home the need to be prepared for travel always so it was a simple matter for me to stop by my den, pick up my jump kit and then make all due speed back to Amber's home. The tension of the hunt was beginning to build in me and, like a wolfhound about to be set to the lure, I was ready to be off and running.

I had just gotten a text from Al-lin that he was in the air and headed for the hunting ground when I pulled into Amber's driveway. She was waiting for me, clad casually in jeans and a forest green sweater, her hair pulled back in a no-nonsense ponytail.

When I pulled up, she gestured for me to roll the window down. Since I had asked her to see about accommodations while I got my gear, I expected a query about possible locations for us to use as a base of operations. Instead, the new wolf just looked at me and smiled, "Turn off the car and lock it, bring your gear. I have a surprise for you."

I started to open my mouth to speak but she walked away, headed back toward the house. Since I had no idea what she was up to, I did as I was told.

I followed Amber through the front door of the house, duffel bag slung over my shoulder, and then through the kitchen to the garage. What I saw there made my mouth fall open for the second time that day. Sitting before me was a fairly new Land Rover; one that had seen some real four-wheeling action, judging by the scratches in the paint. "Where in the world did you come up with this?" I asked, stupefied.

The head of BPI smiled, showing gleaming white teeth, and shrugged eloquently, "You forget that my father is British and that we're loaded. He has several of these," she continued, gesturing at the vehicle, "in the motor pool since he likes to go into the mountains himself when he can get away from work."

"How the heck did you manage to get it here so quick?"

"Well, Ernie, the fellow who takes care of our vehicles, watched me grow up and we are good friends. I asked him if he could get a Land Rover delivered to me, in a hurry, and he was quite obliging."

I grunted as I drew the vehicle's rear door open and deposited my gear in the capacious back section. "I have a few dollars too but I keep forgetting I can use them."

Amber laughed as she threw her bag into the back with mine. The thought crossed my mind that we looked for all the world like a young couple going away for the weekend. The ghost hunter looked across at me, from the passenger side, and must have seen the pensive expression in my eyes. "I wish this were a pleasure trip too," she said and sighed, "but we've got some work to do. Why don't you let me drive the first stretch so you can review what is in there?" She gestured with her chin at the laptop.

I nodded and retrieved the computer and a wireless USB internet modem from the laptop case in the back. The device was fully charged so I should have plenty of time to see the new evidence. A thought occurred to me. "I forgot to ask. Did you find a place for us to stay?"

"Yup. Check your email. Let's get going."

I agreed with that sentiment so, as Amber backed the Land Rover down the driveway and around my Scion, I jacked in the wireless connection and pulled up my email. I managed to keep my mouth from falling open yet again as Amber piloted the SUV down Elmwood, headed to the 190. "I think that I am going to have to hire you, young werewolf. You found a lease cabin in the Adirondack National Forest within spitting distance of Ampersand Lake? I know that your family has a lot of money but that is unnatural."

Amber chuckled. "You presume too much, Black Dog," she said, doing a passable impression of the Sigrun, "actually, this was not a family thing. One of my college roommates is a forest ranger now. I called her and gave her a little story about needing some wilderness retreat time. Hinted that I had heard that the area around Ampersand Lake was beautiful this time of year. She got on her computer and found this cabin. Apparently, it is a hunting lease but the individual who owns the lease passed on this year. Ginger, my old roommate, called the family and they agreed to transfer the lease to me. The wonders of modern technology—they faxed the documents to me and I signed and returned them just before you arrived."

I took my eyes off the computer for a moment. "You took over the lease? For how long?"

Amber smiled mysteriously, "Ninety-nine years."

I started to protest but she silenced me with a raised hand. "Calm down, Zach. I have a trust fund that provides me with a monthly stipend that would make your eyes bulge. My house is paid for and I have, in case you haven't noticed, recently become a werewolf. I'm about to dash off into a hunt as an inexperienced wolf that could very well get me or you or both of us killed. I've made a commitment, before my Goddess, to go off and train as an Oracle with a bunch of warrior maidens. Frankly, I am holding myself together by main force right now, but eventually, if we survive the next few days, I am going to have to sit with all this and get a handle on my new life. That means that I am going to have to be someplace where it is safe for me to run in my other form and quiet enough for me to think. This was an opportunity that I could not let pass."

I paused for a moment, considering. "I've never led a normal life in the Midlands so I cannot imagine what it is like being dragged into my world. It must be a lot to take in and I am feeding it to you at a pace that few people could manage. I cannot make the Other Side go away and, as you say, we have work to do, but, if there is anything I can do to make this easier for you, all you have to do is ask."

Amber took one hand from the wheel and put it over my hand, where it rested on the divider between the seats. She smiled again, but I could see tears bright in her eyes. "What you need to do right now is be all about business because, when I see the care in your eyes, it makes me all teary. I cannot afford to be soft right now; I have to stay mission focused to get through this."

I nodded and softly withdrew my hand. "Mission focus, got it. So, tell me about this cabin."

The ghost hunter sniffed and brushed a hand across her eyes to clear them. "Basically, we will drive into a tiny hamlet called Abbotsville, which apparently sports a service station and convenience store for those who fish Ampersand Lake, turn right on the aptly named Lake Road and head around the lake. I understand that, once we are clear of town, the road is not so great and some of it will be dirt, thus the Land Rover. The town is on private land but, once you have gone up the road for a while, you come back into the national forest. The cabin is set back into the woods a quarter mile off the lake road. It sounds like it will be pretty comfortable for a wilderness retreat—propane for cooking and even has a generator for lights at night if you want them."

"What kind of cabin—log, A-frame, clapboard?

"It's an A-frame. I hear that one of the primary selling features is the huge picture window that looks out into the woods."

"I am sure that it is nice for scenery but it is not so nice when you are hunting a rogue who may be hunting you. Other than that, though, it sounds perfect and I can deal with the glass issue once we get there. "

Amber nodded thoughtfully as she sailed the Land Rover up onto the 90. We were quiet for a little while since we knew we would have to stop at the toll booths shortly. Once we were clear of the toll booth, she punched the Land Rover up to speed and set the cruise control. We would be on the 90 for quite some time before making our exit onto the 81 and heading up into the mountains.

I settled back to review the new information that Al-lin had forwarded to me. My co-pilot and I had already agreed to switch out driving once we hit Syracuse so, in keeping with our commitment to stay focused on the mission; I began to read Amber snatches of text from the morass of documents Al-lin had sent me.

CHAPTER SEVENTEEN

*E*xcept for the huge glass window that occupied the whole front of the A-frame cabin, the place was perfect. Amber and I arrived a little before nightfall.

I parked the truck in front of the cabin and walked the area to stretch my legs, paying close attention to my nose. I'd told Amber to wait for me near the truck. I had no reason to believe that the Beast knew where we were basing our operation but I was not taking any chances. Chastel had already shown that he was going to be a wily opponent and I was not going to give him the chance to get the drop on Amber, or me.

When I was confident that no wolves had been in the area, I rejoined Amber at the Land Rover. "I don't smell anything unusual. I would suggest that we unpack, get something to eat and then Change and do a more thorough survey."

Amber nodded absently, her eyes on the rapidly darkening woods. "Ordinarily, I would be happy to be out here and away from people for a while but right now, I freely admit, it gives me the creeps. After what you told me Chastel did to your GRI researcher . . ."

I struggled not to approach and try to comfort her. One of the things that a new werewolf must learn is how to grow a tough skin. Wolves are predatory carnivores, whether we are talking Canis lupus or werewolf. In order for them to eat, some animal must die. There is no such thing as a vegetarian werewolf although their diet is far more omnivorous than mine. I was lucky I could drink coffee; if I tried to eat some of the things that I have seen werewolves eat, the result would not have been pretty.

Because they are predatory carnivores, when a werewolf goes rogue and begins attacking human beings the results are horrifying to humans. The forensic report on Kyla Tedesco had come with full-color pictures of what had been left of her body. Chastel had made certain that her head and face were undisturbed—a hallmark of his, since he wanted the victim to be identified—but the rest of her body had been so badly mauled that Amber had looked away quickly and swallowed hard when she happened to glance over and see the photos. The werewolf had, of course, eaten the choice chunks of meat, like the liver and heart, but he had been certain to tear up other parts in a calculated way that had nothing to do with frenzy.

Louis Chastel knew who his victim was and who she worked for. The kill had been a cold-blooded challenge to Al-lin of the Greenwood, telling him that there was a monster loose in his demesne and that he had better do something about it. No wonder Al-lin had been so enraged that he had almost called a Hunt, damage to the Midlands be damned

"Amber," I said, at last, "you can look at those pictures one of two ways. You can view them and feel fear at the awful thing that did them or you can look and say to yourself: no more. That last one is what I have to do, have had to do, too many times over the course of my career."

The red-headed wolf looked me squarely in the face. "And it does not scare you?"

I shook my head. "It scares me plenty. No being, human or

Black Dog, wants to end up like that and there is always that possibility with every hunt. The fear of being eaten is one of the most primal fears that a sentient being with a corporeal form can know."

Night was settling in and I could barely see her as she dropped her head. She had taken her hair out of the ponytail for a while and it dropped across her face. "How do you deal with that fear? I can stand and fight people with guns and knives but this . . . this is different."

"Yes, it is. This is one of those times when knowing how to access your wolf without Changing is good. You should remember that she is smart and fast and she will do everything that she is instinctually geared to do, to keep you alive. One of the mistakes that new wolves make, once they have sure control over their inner animal, is to disregard the animal part. They walk around in a wolf's form but they think like a person and pay no attention to the instincts of the animal that they can become. Sometimes, it is those instincts that can save your life."

Amber nodded slowly. "It's a fine line, isn't it? You have to bring the human to the fore or you are out of control but you really need those animal instincts to help you survive."

There was not much I could add to that so we grabbed our gear, moved onto the hardwood deck that wrapped all the way around the structure and into the dark cabin, sniffing carefully to be sure that there was no trap before opening the door and going inside.

Amber moved past me and flipped another switch. Apparently, the house batteries still had enough charge to provide some electricity. Twin lamps, in the middle of the great room, sprang to life and revealed the space to us. The cabin was set up to highlight the tall arc of glass that showed nothing but dark night at the moment but which would reveal the wood in all its glory when the sun rose again.

As we walked out into the great room, we noted a staircase

made from split logs that led up to a sleeping loft. We made our way slowly up the stairs, and found, to our surprise, the loft contained two queen beds and a massive oak chest of drawers so we did not have to worry about any awkwardness in regards to sleeping arrangements and had plenty of room to store our sparse gear.

Amber glanced at me from across the loft. "Looks pretty comfy. I will, eventually, have to explore ways that I can have an actual refrigerator out here without wrecking the silence but, for now, the icebox looks serviceable and we can go into Abbotsville in the morning and get some ice if you think we will need it."

I held up the little cooler with my food supply. "I prefer my meat unspoiled."

Amber chuckled but the humor seemed strained. "A few days ago, I would have thought that was repulsive. Now I find myself thinking that I like my meat still warm, with the blood still in it." She shuddered involuntarily.

Again, I restrained the urge to go to her and offer comfort. Instead, I sat on the edge of the bed that I had staked out, the one nearest the staircase entrance, and I gestured for Amber to sit across from me. She seemed reluctant but complied with my wish after a moment. I gazed directly into her eyes and noted the gold rims around her green pupils. "You are hungry, aren't you?"

The ghost hunter nodded absently. "And control is harder for you when you are hungry, right?"

Amber's eyes glistened as she nodded again.

"And you are afraid that you are not going to be able to do this, that you are going to lose control?"

The beautiful redhead eyed me intently, "Yes," she murmured, "but it is more than that. I am afraid that, even if I do manage to keep control it is always going to be this hard. That I am going to have to live out all the years ahead of me, struggling with this nature that I did not even ask for."

"What was done to you is a crime, Amber. Under the Charter,

it is punishable by death, given the use of necromancy. You are truly the victim here but you cannot allow that it's-not-fair thinking to overwhelm you or you will, eventually, erode your control to the point that you do lose it. I know it is hard but you have to keep your head up, remember who the human in you is and get to know the other side as well. If you do that, you will reach a point where the two sides integrate and control will become less an issue."

Amber drew a deep shuddering breath. "It will get easier?"

I nodded carefully, "It will. Someday you will look back on these first few days and wonder why you found it so difficult. Remember, I have known a lot of werewolves in my day. I know what I am talking about."

The yellow rings in her pupils expanded slightly. "I need to know how to get in touch with the wolf without bringing it through. Like you were talking about when we got here. She is there, I can feel her all the time, and I need to know how to communicate with her."

I eyed my charge curiously. "Why?"

Amber shrugged. "I am not sure really. I just feel that if I can talk to her, maybe I can, I don't know, negotiate."

"That is a skill that most werewolves don't start to learn until they have been Changed for a while but let's see if you can do it. Close your eyes."

Her eyelids dropped instantly and she automatically assumed an upright posture.

CHAPTER EIGHTEEN

I waited a few moments for my student to settle then continued, "Good, now go through the exercise that I taught you to ground yourself."

I looked at my companion with mundane and magical senses and could see her breathing deepen and her energy settle as she sank into a calmer state. "Very good, Amber, now remember this feeling. It is something you can access when you feel like your control is weak and you need to settle. Got that?"

"Now, I want you to open your inner eyes and leave your outer eyes closed. What do you see?"

"The wolf, she is standing next to me."

"Okay, what does she want? Remember that she is a wolf and she will not speak to you in words. Look at her body, the way her ears lay against her head, the position of her tail, the way her fur lays. Anything that will give you a clue as to what she is trying to communicate."

This was the part where the exercise usually fell apart since the human part of a new werewolf did not have the awareness of body language that the wolf did. Until the two had been together for a while, the human had trouble interpreting the language of the wolf. Nevertheless, I could see that Amber was concentrating on taking in the position of her wolf.

Abruptly, her eyes sprang open and she exclaimed, "Oh!" as she stared into the distance in front of her, her eyes still locked in the Otherworld.

"What is it, Amber?" I asked gently.

The young woman continued to stare before her as though I had not spoken but, after a moment, she replied, "The wolf. She wants to come in because she knows that I am hungry and she thinks we should go hunt."

I frowned. "How do you know this?"

Amber shrugged in her trance. "Not sure. It's like I am hearing her in my head. Not really words but . . . images, flashes, impressions."

I had never seen this in a werewolf before but, then again, I had never worked with an untrained Oracle before. I would have to take her at her word and see how this played out. "Alright, can you send a message back to her?"

It was Amber's turn to frown. "Not sure but I can try."

"Tell the wolf that you are going to feed in this form and later you will run with her."

My cohort's brow crinkled for a moment and then she turned as though she were turning to a wolf standing next to her. After several moments had elapsed, the subtle tension that had filled her body since our conversation had begun relaxed and Amber sighed deeply in her semi-trance. "I think she understands. She is still with me but her presence is not so . . . imperative."

I nodded, eyebrows rising in surprise. "Excellent. You can reverse the procedure and come back to full consciousness now."

Amber took a minute to return to normal awareness but, once she was back and her eyes were clear and focused in the loft where we sat, I noted that the yellow rings had disappeared from her pupils.

* * *

I HAD NEVER HEARD of a werewolf that could actually talk, in a manner of speaking, with its wolf but it seemed that Amber had accomplished this feat. She fulfilled her word to her wolf and went downstairs immediately to eat. I joined her in the little kitchen and had a snack as well then, once we had digested some of the meal, I went into the entrance hallway.

I cracked the door so that we could get out without dealing with door handles and lay my clothes neatly on a kitchen counter, Changing to my true form. Amber had gone upstairs to accomplish the same thing and a few minutes later, the scent of werewolf permeated the house. I did not have a clock available but I would bet that she had made the Change in less than five minutes. It seemed that she was getting quicker each time she transformed and she seemed to be experiencing far less discomfort than in her earlier Changes.

The red-tipped wolf made her way cautiously down the stairs and bumped my shoulder to let me know that she was ready to go. I nudged the door open with my nose and Amber preceded me out the entry. We moved into the forest that surrounded the cabin and I turned giving a sharp bark on a particular key, reaching into the fire of my spirit for power. My eyes burned crimson red and wards flared to life in my magical sight. I gave a satisfied huff. Amber's wolf strode up beside me and stared for a moment, then lowered her head and made a noise that sounded suspiciously like a satisfied chortle.

One of the disadvantages of running in a non-human form is that you cannot use the usual methods of magic. Gesture and spoken word or chant work well for human beings but not for a hellhound. Magic surrounds those of my kind but it is the magic of necromancy, of dealing with the dead and, if called for, bringing death. I found that I wanted to be able to use some of my runic spells in my Dog form and had consulted with the

Sigrun about how to accomplish that task. We did a lot of experimentation and eventually I learned to key certain workings to a very specific sound; a bark, growl, or howl, at a particular vibration, would invoke the spell I was trying to cast.

As with all things, the Mother of Runes had drilled me until I could get the spell I wanted, when I wanted it, every time. If Chastel should discover where our camp lay, I had just encircled it with a ring of the twenty-four runes of the Elder Futhark. He would be in for a quite nasty surprise if he attempted to penetrate the wards.

Despite my tension, I enjoyed the time out on that cool night. The scent of pine, intermingled with the green, leafy smell of the deciduous trees, created a heady perfume as a backdrop for my search. There was a thick overcast that dulled the light of the nearly three-quarter moon but, despite the lack of illumination, I could feel the slippery lichens on the rocks beneath my paws and scent the honeyed odor of clover as I crossed open clearings. I knew that, when the sun came up in the morning, my eyes would be greeted by the sight of a New York forest in full color before the leaves dropped and the land settled in for winter.

Amber, striding smoothly next to me, seemed to pick up on my mood, lifting her head and scenting deeply as we made our way down a game trail several miles from the cabin. Her ears swiveled and she gave a curious look as a screech owl gave its grating call and took flight from a tree to our left. Dog and wolf melded into the foliage as one, waiting to see what had flushed the owl. Moments later, a black bear ambled onto the game trail and then crashed into the brush not twenty feet in front of us. Amber ghosted back onto the trail once the bear had passed and we resumed our search.

My wolf companion had been doing very well in the woods, so well, in fact, that I had encouraged her to go off and cover part of our search grid on her own earlier. Despite the abundant presence of game animals, Amber's wolf had stayed on task, seemingly intent on the job of finding the rogue werewolf. She had just rejoined me when we ran into the bear and I was contemplating sending her off to cover another section of the wilderness when I smelled it.

My head and hackles came up at the same time Amber's did, the pungent scent hitting us both at the same time, carried on the downhill breeze. We turned as one animal in the direction of the smell. It was weak but it was definitely there and, though I had never scented Louis Chastel, there was no local werewolf or werewolf pack that could account for the musk on the wind. Syracuse pack had moved closer to the New York City area a couple of years previously and ran in the Catskills and I'd had Allin quietly warn the Buffalo wolves to stay out of the Adirondacks until further notice.

Amber might have been a new wolf but she responded according to her animal instincts and did not allow the human to slow her down. She moved, slowly and quietly into the brush to my right, protecting my flank as we moved up the sharp rise toward the source of the smell. As we climbed, she angled her ascent sideways drawing further from me. Given the weakness of the scent cone coming down the mountainside, it was unlikely that Chastel was still there but, if he was, there was no way that he could engage both of us in a single charge.

I crested the rise, and came into an open field, keeping my head low, as Amber stopped and waited silently under a bunchberry bush. Her back legs were bunched under her and I knew that she could rocket to my aid in a matter of seconds if necessary. It occurred to me that it would be very easy for me to get used to having her at my back.

The clearing was covered in clover with devil's paintbrush poking up in random clusters. The clouds had shredded as we stalked the scent and faint moonlight shone through as I made my way slowly across the space, my belly to the ground and ears pricked forward at full alert. Ahead of me, on a knoll, something moved sluggishly in the cool night breeze. My nose told me that this was the source of the smell that I was following.

I stopped, extending my senses, looking for a booby trap. The forest was quiet to untrained ears but, to me, it laid out a pastiche of sensory input. Amber still lay, like a missile prepared for launch, under her bush. Various mice and other small rodents scurried away from me, using the clover as cover. A rabbit lay quivering with terror under some nearby sedge. The screech owl we had heard earlier sat in a silver maple, watching the scene with wide night eyes.

Magical senses came into play but I felt not the slightest hint of magic burning in the still night. It was possible that Chastel had left a spell trap that would only 'detonate' in proximity to a certain Black Dog but that sort of spell, sneaky as it is, still left a trace for those who knew how to look . . . most of the time. I knew how to look and I was reasonably certain that there was no trap. I inched forward, one slow step at a time, willing my body to relax as I moved toward my goal.

At length, I topped the knoll and saw that the source of the scent was a rag, tied to a branch and stuck into the ground. I approached cautiously and noted that there was a note pinned to the ground in front of the makeshift scent flag. The text was short:

KNOW YOUR PREY

CHAPTER NINETEEN

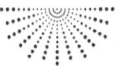

I chuffed and Amber came out of hiding at a trot instead of a dead run. She approached the flag, glanced at the note and the look in her golden eyes told me that she was contemplating marking territory around the note in a very graphic way. I confess that I had a momentary urge to lift my leg on the thing too but common sense kicked in and took over from the Dog's instinct. I placed my nose against the cloth and inhaled deeply, several times, carving Chastel's scent into my memory for later.

Amber watched and, when I had done, followed my example.

We made our circuitous way back to the cabin and, after I had dropped the wards and we had done a thorough inspection of the area around the cabin, went back indoors. I re-activated the wards to prevent any nighttime surprises, pulled the door carefully to with my jaws and Amber and I made our way up the stairs to the sleeping loft. Not even bothering to change back to our human forms, we curled up on our respective beds and dropped into dreamless sleep, exhausted from the night's efforts

* * *

As USUAL, I woke within a couple of hours. Light was just beginning to filter into the cabin from the coming dawn and I huffed contentedly, curling up for a moment and placing my tail over my nose, reluctant to move from the comfort of the soft bed and the view out the A-frame's massive picture window. I do not require a lot of sleep but, when I am on a hunt, particularly a stressful one like this one, the cumulative effects of that stress begin to make me feel tired even when I have slept. Eventually, the fatigue would culminate in my sleeping an entire night away.

I sighed, wishing I could afford that luxury, but Chastel had demonstrated last night that he knew I was there and that I was after him. From here on out, there would be very little time for sleeping; I needed to get into some of the local areas where people lived today—Abbotsville and Beresford and, perhaps, Saranac Lake—and see if I could get a bead on where the rogue's human form had been hanging out or, better yet, where he was staying.

Of course, it was possible that Chastel was living rough. As a werewolf, he would have no trouble feeding himself and he came from a time when woodland survival skills had been necessary just to stay alive. He could construct basic shelter and knew where to look for water and how to get a fire going for the times when he was not in his fur coat.

Still, my survey of Chastel and everything that was known about him back in the Academy had given me a better than average feel for his personality. He had amassed quite a fortune over the years, stolen from his victims and others, and his modus operandi was to enter an area, set himself up in sumptuous quarters, get the lay of the land and then begin taking prey. He had developed a taste for comfortable accommodations and had learned to speak and behave like a man of leisure, setting aside the simple country boy that he had been.

Amber shifted on her bed and I glanced away from the view for a moment and then riveted my eyes back on the bed. At some point in the night, my companion had shifted back into her human form but was still laying, as a wolf would, curled into a ball on the bed, stark naked. How on Earth had she managed to shift back without waking?

I edged down off my bed as silently as I could and took hold of a comforter at the foot of the bed, drawing it over her naked form without disturbing her. There was no way that I could avoid getting a full view of the lovely curve of her hip and buttocks and the strong, taut musculature of her back.

Even in my Dog form, I gulped and tried to pull my mind to other things but my eyes betrayed me, moving fondly over her body as though we had been together for years, following the angle of her shoulder down to the gentle slope of a breast, hidden becomingly beneath her arm. Her red hair splayed out around her head in a halo lit by the strengthening light of day.

With an almost physical effort, I dropped the comforter over her shoulders and retreated, backing away slowly and then making my way downstairs. I Changed and retrieved my clothes from the night before, moving into the bathroom to wash up in shockingly cold water from a hand pump at the sink. The chills crawling across my skin did nothing to settle the fire that burned in me. I stood, resting my hands on the old porcelain basin that served as a sink, and stared into the mirror past the hand pump.

What the hell was wrong with me? I had been without steady female companionship most of my life and it had never really bothered me until now. I had, of course, had longer relationships but, moving around as I had, being what I was and doing what I did, it was not easy for me to form any sort of lasting bond much less one that would last more than the length of an assignment.

Granted, I was now semi-settled in Buffalo and it seemed unlikely that I would be moved anytime soon but I found myself enamored of a new werewolf. In my business that just was not done. A new wolf, even one who was doing as well as Amber, could encounter something in the life that it could not deal with and then have to be put down. That was my job and, already, I knew that I would have a lot of trouble if Amber should go rogue.

My Dog was actually thinking of the woman more and more in terms of mate and the human part of me was not far behind. Only my training and the fact that Amber had made it clear that she needed some time to assimilate into her new life had kept me from trying to get closer to her. I heaved a long shuddering sigh and took some deep breaths, trying to tamp down this new fire that burned within me.

I would probably have been alright if Amber had not chosen that exact time to appear in the bathroom door, the comforter wrapped around her and her hair a radiant mess around her face. "Are you alright, Zach?" she asked, concern etched on her face, "I woke up and you weren't there and . . . I smelled something. You don't smell right. Are you hurt?"

I tried to shrug it off, to say something flippant and lighten the mood but my tongue just would not seem to cooperate as I gazed at her, limned in early morning light, her shoulders bare above the comforter. I wanted to bridge the gap between us, take her in my arms, muss her hair even more prettily and not come out of the cabin for days. Something of what I was feeling must have shown on my face; Amber took a step into the room, her eyes wide and rimmed with gold.

"Damn it, Amber, don't come any closer. I think I need a cold shower and a good run."

Amber shook her head and when she spoke, her voice was husky with suppressed emotion, "No, Zach, that is not what you need. This is what you need."

She dropped the comforter and any semblance of control left my mind. I cleared the space between us in two long strides, swept her up in my arms and carried her to the loft.

* * *

AFTERWARD, as we lay spent and sweaty beneath the sheets, Amber's head nestled on my shoulder, she turned her intense green eyes on me. "Are you okay?" she asked, in the same tone she had used when she had sought me out earlier.

I smiled and kissed her softly before replying. "I'm better than okay. I am . . ." Words failed me and I tightened my arms around her.

"Mated?" she asked, trying to keep her voice light. The anxiety in the question startled me and I drew away enough to look her full in the face.

"I've never been mated but, yes, I am pretty sure that is what happened. You?" I asked with some asperity.

She nodded slowly, her eyes full of unshed tears. "I never thought I would have to become a werewolf to find someone who wanted me just for me. My wolf has been telling me that you were the one for a while now but my human half was not as quick to get it. As I've said, in the human world I was always dodging men who were stalking me for my money or for my looks or both."

I tightened my arms around her again. "Anyone stalking you now is going to be in for a big surprise. Pulling on a werewolf's tail is dangerous business."

She grinned at me, her face open and at ease for the first time since the bite that had Changed her, then rolled playfully on top of me. I did not protest when she whispered, "The only one I want to play with my tail is you."

* * *

DUTY DID EVENTUALLY RE-ASSERT ITSELF. Despite the delay, Amber and I were out the door before noon that day. After our exertions of the morning, I had gotten a fire going in the wood stove in the kitchen— much simpler when you can simply summon fire to light the logs—and warmed water so that we could bathe properly. Bath time had almost resulted in another trip up the stairs but we were stern with each other and managed our morning ablutions without too much teasing.

Once we were bathed and dressed, Amber and I mounted up and drove the Land Rover down the long drive and onto the lake road. We made our way down the curvy lane to Abbotsville and stopped at the run-down building that housed the convenience store and post office. There were a couple of older men sitting on the porch, rocking gently in bentwood rockers that looked—much like the men who sat in them—like they had seen better days.

I glanced through the hazy glass at the front of the business and noted that, despite the remoteness of the location, the store actually had some food supplies that might come in useful at some point and a huge freezer unit for ice at the back. A Coca-Cola sign, circa 1940s, hung crookedly over the cash register, just inside the door.

CHAPTER TWENTY

I was expecting to do my detective thing but Amber walked up, propped her arms on the porch rail and lit the two up with her best smile. I felt warmth flash over me, even though the smile was not directed at me, and the two gentlemen on the porch suddenly sat up a little straighter. It did not hurt that my new lover had dressed in jeans that accentuated the smooth lines of her legs and a silk blouse that dipped just low enough to get most men's attention.

"Good afternoon," she said, somehow managing to make both the men on the porch feel included in the greeting, "I just took the lease on a cabin down the road. I am new to the area so I thought I would stop in and introduce myself. Amber Morgan," she said, as she climbed up onto the porch and shook hands with both the codgers. I hung back, more than a little amused, and watched her work.

The two men appeared to be brothers so I instantly dubbed them Brother 1 and Brother 2. Brother 1 looked the new werewolf up and down with undisguised admiration and said, "Cabin down the road, you say. Whereabouts?"

Amber described our drive to him and both porch sitters

nodded. "Yup, that would be old man Wrighter's place. Or used to be. I heard he passed on," the other brother, the one who had not spoken yet, stated.

Amber nodded and looked appropriately solemn. "That is what I was told, yes. Bad news for one person, good news for another, I guess. The cabin came open right as I was looking for a place with some privacy."

Both old guys' eyes shifted to me and Amber laughed lightly, "Well, yes, my sweetie has something to do with that but mostly I was looking for a place where I could come and write."

Both brothers looked at the potential celebrity with renewed attention. Amber played it perfectly, as though she were taking them into her confidence, and spun a story about collecting ghost stories from all over New York State.

Brother 2 eyed Amber closely and then burst out, "I'll be damned! "Scuse my language, miss. I knew I had seen you somewhere before. You're one of those ghost hunters, right?"

Amber covered her surprise well. There was no point in denying her affiliation so she said, "Yes, I am. I run a group called Buffalo Paranormal Investigations."

Brother 2 was a big fan of the BPI website and had recognized Amber from pictures there. Apparently, he used information from the ghost hunting site in his ongoing arguments with Brother 1 about the paranormal.

The two looked as though they were about to get back into that very argument until Amber skillfully diverted them. "Well, I am glad to know that someone appreciates the website but I wonder if I could ask you a question? Nothing to do with ghost hunting really but I am looking for an old friend that I heard was living up this direction."

Amber walked to the edge of the porch and handed them a recent security video photo of Chastel that Al-lin had supplied. The photo had been cropped to make it look like a portrait shot. Both men looked hard at the picture but both shook their heads.

Amber made polite small talk for a few minutes and promised to stop by and see the two brothers, Joshua and Jay Edgerton, when she had more time to chat. She asked where the two brothers would go if they were looking for someone in the area and they both allowed as how they would head over to Saranac Lake and check in at the Half Moon Café on Main Street. Once the new werewolf had disengaged herself and given the brothers her phone number, telling them to call if they should happen to see Chastel, we dropped into the Land Rover and turned in the direction of Saranac Lake.

* * *

AMBER and I made the drive from Abbotsville to Saranac Lake along State Route 3, a road that managed to run from one place in the Adirondacks to another in a fairly straight line.

"I screwed up this morning, didn't I? I've put you in a really awkward position."

I started to deny it but she put her hand softly on my leg and looked directly at me. "No. Let me talk. What I said this morning was true. It seems silly that I had to become a werewolf to find someone who accepted me for who I am. I made a decision based on impulse and stress but, now that I think on it, I realize that I have been really selfish."

I took her hand and squeezed, keeping my eyes on the road as I replied, "Not selfish, really. Neither of us thought it through. This is what happens when you have instincts as well as logic and intuition to rely on. Sometimes, the animal part has other ideas and drags the more human part along with it. We cannot undo what is done and, honestly, I would not undo it, even if I could."

Green eyes stared at me intensely. "Seriously?"

I nodded, glancing over at her so she could see my face. "You commented once that mine must be a lonely life. You are right. I have never had anyone in my life for more than a few months, in all the time I have been alive . . ."

Amber's face tightened and I could hear the stress in her words as she interrupted, "But a new wolf, Zach? How the hell are you going to explain that to your superiors? Just yesterday, you were coaching me on how to deal with my new state and that was simply because I had allowed myself to get too hungry. I am smart enough to know that I have a long way to go before I am really comfortable with this change in my life and a lot could go wrong."

Again, I took my eyes off the road for a moment. I could see unshed tears, luminous in her eyes. "I have been around a long time, Amber. If I thought you were going to go rogue, I would have been a lot more circumspect in my behavior toward you and I suspect that the Dog would have been much more recalcitrant too. He seems to be able to smell that sort of thing. Yes, it is a risk, but I don't think that you can be with someone unless you are willing to take a chance."

My lover brushed knuckles across her eyes and they came away wet. I wanted to kiss those tears from her hand but continued driving, uncertain what more to say. Eventually, Amber drew a deep breath and I could feel her centering and grounding herself as I had taught her. After a moment, she said quietly, "If you are willing to take this risk, then so am I. Now that I have crossed the line, I cannot see going back but you have to swear to me that you will keep the promise you made me."

I looked at her, puzzled for a moment, then remembered. She gazed steadily at me, her eyes imploring. I felt the tension in my shoulders, resistance to what she asked of me, but I also felt the Dog rise in me, a creature of the Otherworld, born and bred to keep humans and other beings safe from rogue werewolves. I felt the fire come into my eyes involuntarily but Amber did not flinch from that searing red gaze. I found my voice after a moment, "I made you a promise, Amber, and I will keep it if I must."

She smiled softly and leaned over, kissing me softly on the cheek. "My promise to you is that I will do all that I can to keep you from ever having to fulfill that oath."

Silence settled over the Land Rover again but this time it was a silence of contentment.

* * *

THE TOWN of Saranac Lake was founded in the early 1800s and was most famous as the site of a sanitarium for the treatment of tuberculosis in the latter part of that century. Our destination, the Half Moon Café, was a two-story square red brick structure with a porch that swept across the front of the first floor. The porch had been painted white but was roofed in shingles of a vivid "moon" blue. The posts that supported the roof had been lathed and, though they were predominantly white had color highlights added at intervals to increase their interest. The handrails leading up to the porch had been painted to match.

Amber and I walked into the restaurant and ducked into the empty bar on the left. A long mirror ran the entire length of the dark mahogany bar and a nondescript fellow with glasses that magnified his eyes in a disconcerting way was busily drying glasses as we seated ourselves on stools.

While he retrieved our drink order, we quickly discovered that the bartender went by Red and that he was a transplant from Buffalo who had fallen for a local girl during a summer vacation from college and never returned to the Nickel City. He and his wife made ends meet working a variety of jobs in and around the area. Amber and I maintained the cover that she had invented while talking to the Edgerton brothers; we were new to the area, had leased a cabin over near Ampersand Lake and were just getting to know the area so thought we would come in to see the lovely Saranac Lake.

Amber and I had developed a decent rapport with Red until

she pulled out the picture of Chastel. I could see from his body language that he was about to clam up as he spat, "This guy is a friend of yours?"

I changed direction immediately to avoid losing a potential witness, "Okay, okay," I said, affecting a sly grin, "you got us. The bastard owes me money. I am inclined to collect it from him or take it out of his hide, one of the two."

Red seemed to accept that as a legitimate reason to be pursuing Chastel and his demeanor opened up a little. As it happened, Chastel had not been making a secret of his presence in the area and he had been anything but pleasant to the locals, treating them like servants and complaining everywhere he went. Red expressed the opinion that the man needed a good beating to teach him how to treat people.

The break I was looking for came after Red had ended his tirade. "I heard that he is living up in your area somewhere— Ampersand Lake—but over on the westside of the lake, some- where around White Lily Pond and Madison Mountain. You might check with Molly Redbow, down at the Fine Arts Studio, couple of blocks down from here. Word is that your boy dropped a bundle buying some fine art reproductions for his place."

Amber and I thanked the bartender and Amber gave him a card with her emergency number on it in case Chastel should be seen in the area. After we had made a little more small talk, we thanked Red for the drinks and the information and headed up onto Main Street once again. We were sure to leave a good tip for the bartender; he had shown us pictures of his three children, one of whom was in college now.

CHAPTER TWENTY-ONE

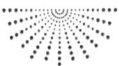

ine Arts Studio was, as Red had promised, exactly two blocks away, a small clapboard building tucked in between two larger brick structures. The studio was a small store that specialized in fine art reproductions and Amber and I roamed the surprisingly large sales floor, moving from one perfectly lighted print to another until someone came out of the back room in response to the door chime. I guessed that, as winter approached and the tourists fled, whoever oversaw the place did not feel any urgency to get onto the floor and sell.

The young woman who came out of the back room was Native American, most likely Iroquois, in this part of the country. She was shorter than Amber and not nearly as lithe but she carried herself with notable physical grace. Her hair was raven black and she had a pleasant open face. She smiled as she approached us but I noted a slight magical tension in the air as she made her way across the sales floor. I heard Amber inhale deeply as she sensed it and looked to me.

I stepped between the seemingly innocuous salesperson and Amber as I murmured a charm of protection and powered it with just enough energy to make it obvious that I was a practitioner too. The woman stopped three-quarters of the way to meeting us and held out her hand.

I felt her extend her senses and touch the edge of the delicate shield I had projected. "Either you come in peace or you have no power to stop me from walking through this protection like tissue paper," she said in a clear, almost tenor voice. Her eyebrows rose in question.

"I come in peace but I am quite capable of defending myself if I must." I amped the energy in the shield just enough to show that I could be serious and angled it to deflect any incoming attack.

The young woman smiled again. "Ah, yes, so I see. Declare yourself, please."

I bowed slightly, hoping that this was not going to come down to a duel. "I am Zachary Collins, initiate of the Order of the Valkyrja, and this is my companion, Amber Morgan." I did not make this earnest young woman as a hostile so I took a calculated risk and dropped my shields.

The shopkeeper smiled and immediately lowered her own defenses. "I am Molly Redbow. I was trained in the old ways of my people by my grandmother who was trained by her grandmother who was trained by her grandmother through all the generations of my clan. We have been healers for all those generations but we have also protected the People from spirits that mean the People harm."

"I own this store," Molly continued, "I inherited it from the Englishwoman who owned it previously. She was very old when her people sought me out. I could not save her life but I eased her suffering and she bestowed this little piece of her estate on me. It gives me a place to live, some money in my pocket and a place where my people can always find me. You have spoken the truth but you have not told me everything. I smell the wolf on this one." Molly gestured with her chin toward Amber.

I explained Amber's infection, my own role as Black Dog for the area and why we were there. As I did so, Molly began to nod.

"I am sorry if I seemed overly cautious when you came in but I am certain that I ran into your rogue a couple of weeks ago. The experience was not pleasant."

I handed Molly the picture of Chastel and she glanced at it briefly. "Yes, that is the one."

Amber stepped to my side and asked gently, "What happened?"

Molly's expressive eyebrows drew in as the skin around her eyes tightened. "This Chastel came in here a couple of weeks ago and, as soon as he recognized my magic, threw a nasty shield in my face. I thought it was going to come down to combat for a couple of minutes but, after saying some things I simply will not repeat, he just dropped the shield and stormed out. Then, he turned around and placed an Internet order for some prints."

"In any event, he has made himself known all along the main drag here and everyone I have spoken too would spit on him if they were not so afraid of him. It seems clear to me that he wanted everyone to remember him. He must have known that you would come looking for him when people started to disappear out in the wilds."

It was my turn to quirk an eyebrow. Molly laughed nervously, then explained that her contacts with the tribe had been keeping her apprised of what was happening in the wilderness area and that at least two of them, poor people hunting to supplement their food supplies for winter, had spotted the werewolf. Fortunately, both had been downwind and had remained still until the danger passed.

I quailed when I heard how close some of her people had come to be victims. "I know that your people need to hunt, Molly, but I am going to ask you to pass the word and keep them out of the forest until I can bring Chastel in. If it is going to cause them to starve this winter, let me know. I have resources that can be sure they are fed this winter. Will you do that for me?"

Molly nodded solemnly. "Give me your word that the people

will be fed and I will do all I can to keep them out of the forest." She held out her hand to me.

I placed my hand lightly over hers and gave my word. I had the means to feed the local tribal folk if needed but I was certain that Al-lin would pitch in as well. He would never allow children to go hungry, especially due to a rogue.

"The last thing that I need from you, Molly, is the address of the cabin where those prints were delivered."

Molly looked at me as though I had lost my mind. "Why would you go there? He is obviously setting a trap for you."

I smiled, a touch wolfishly, "Oh, I am certain that it is a trap but, sometimes, you have to spring the trap to flush the hunter."

The shopkeeper shrugged eloquently and gave me the address. Amber and I exchanged cards with her and promised to keep her apprised of the situation as it unfolded.

* * *

ONCE WE WERE OUTSIDE, I pulled out my cell phone and had Al-lin on the line in moments.

"So, Black Dog, how goes the hunt?" the dry voice greeted me.

"It is about to get interesting, boss," I replied. I outlined my conversation with Molly Redbow and gave him the address she had handed me. I could hear computer keys clicking in the background and surmised that Al-lin had brought Kevin Chen into the field with him.

After a moment, Al-lin spoke. "Kevin is here with me, in case you had not guessed. He has cross-referenced the address, gotten coordinates, and pulled the cabin up on Google Earth. That will do for now. Before we assault the place, I will see if we can get some clear satellite photos. Even Kevin cannot get me access to the spy satellites but I do have a contact with NSA who owes me a favor after we did a job for him. I am fairly certain we can get some good pictures of the place before we go forward. How soon do you want to move?"

I glanced at the sky, orange red in the west as the sun sank behind the mountains surrounding me on all sides. "It is getting dark already. I know your guys have night vision but I would hate to set them loose on a potential werewolf lair with no peripheral vision. How about first light tomorrow morning?"

"That would be suitable," Al-lin responded, "what do you think the chances are that Chastel will be there?"

"Minimal," I replied, "but not beyond the realm of possibility. The Beast is an arrogant bastard and he might just want to teach you a lesson about meddling with him."

I could hear the heat in the Faery prince's voice as he replied, "The furry bastard is going to learn that he is not the only one in these woods with claws. I will be sure that I have my people properly armored and armed and I will be along for magical countermeasures, just in case."

"You also need to be aware," Al-lin continued, "that calling this building a cabin is something of a misnomer. Edward is pulling up county tax information and, according to the land description, the 'cabin' is about 4000 square feet and has three bedrooms and a master suite larger than my first dwelling in the Midlands."

"Typical Chastel," I replied, "he is known for finding the nicest places to live that he can afford and, after all these years, he can afford just about anything he wants. I will go in for a very close look tonight and will be sure to relay the information to you before dawn comes."

Concern tinged Al-lin's voice as he replied, "You are aware that this is likely a trap? Everything you have told me indicates that Chastel wanted us to find him in this lair."

I nodded to myself and noted that Amber was watching me closely. "I am aware that it could be a trap but it is the only lead we have right now."

"And, if the Beast is actually hunting you?" Al-lin asked, his tone demanding a good answer

I smiled. His tone always became more imperious when he was worried about something or someone. It is nice to know you are a valued employee. "You know me, Al-lin. I have been hunting rogues for a long time, I am trained in magic that will be foreign to Chastel and, I hope, harder for him to counter. If he is coming for me, I am going to give him a fight.

"My biggest advantage though is that I have allies. Remember, he is used to working against the normal Black Dog—a being that works in solitude. I am not going to engage him or let him engage me unless I am sure that I have support available."

Al-lin sighed. "I guess that is all I can ask. Be careful out there tonight, Black Dog, and I will speak to you before daybreak."

I signed off and then started the Land Rover, pulled it out of the tight parking space and headed back to the cabin.

CHAPTER TWENTY-TWO

"*W*hat do you mean, you want to go reconnoiter Chastel's cabin alone?" my lover demanded.

"Just what I said, Amber. I cannot take you with me. It's far too dangerous."

She looked at me as though I were carrying a live, writhing rat in my mouth. "Too dangerous?" she said quietly, "I've been bitten by a spirit wolf, engaged in what turned out to be mortal combat with a Valkyrja, and gone through the Change early. I've managed to impress the Sigrun of the Valkyrja but you want me to sit around here and twiddle my thumbs. What exactly is it that you think I am incapable of doing?"

"You do not have nearly enough woodcraft to go stalking an experienced werewolf, Amber."

She started to reply but I held up my hands to stop her. "Don't get me wrong, you are doing very well and your instincts are great but we cannot afford to give ourselves away with a small misstep. I have been doing this for many years and I have made my share of mistakes believe me. The wounds healed long ago, but believe me, I still bear the mental scars."

Amber flinched but refused to back down. "I cannot learn if

you are not willing to take me into the field, Zach. I was under the impression that we started a partnership when we came together this morning."

I wanted to touch her but the anger and hurt on her face stopped me. "We did. We are pack now, Amber, and pack takes care of its own. It would kill me if something happened to you."

She seemed to soften a little at that but she turned my statement back on me. "And how am I supposed to feel if you go off and get killed and I am not even there to try to help or get someone else to help?"

I didn't have a ready answer for that so she continued. "If I am honest, I have to admit that part of the reason that I want to go is that I do not want to stay here by myself. I know that the Beast is out there and, if we have figured out where he is, then there is some chance that he has worked out where we are. I don't have the skills to fight him and I might not be able to evade him and, from what you have said, it would be just like him to try and use me against you."

I looked at her, mouth open, and realized that she had very likely stumbled over the Beast's strategy. How could I have missed that? It was classic Chastel: never fight fair when you can fight dirty and one of his favorite ways to fight dirty was to place the other fighter at a disadvantage. I looked out at the darkness beyond the huge picture window of the cabin and knew that my lover was absolutely right.

"I am an idiot, Amber, please forgive me. We need to get you out of here right now."

She looked at me, green eyes bright, gold rims appearing as she detected my stress, "Should I Change?"

I shook my head. "No time. We need to get clear of this place and get you to a safe spot. I am thinking that we might have to drive over to the airstrip where Al-lin has stationed himself and get you into protective custody."

Amber opened her mouth to protest but I silenced her with a

kiss. "Pack takes care of its own, Amber. I cannot fight if I know you are in danger. Any more than you could if the situation was reversed . . . I think."

She looked deep into my eyes and must have seen the fear for her there. "You think correctly. I could not let anything happen to you."

I heaved a sigh of relief. "Okay, then let's get out of here." I extended my hand, she took it and then all hell broke loose.

* * *

ACCORDING to the rules of mundane science, a person should be the same size and weight in wolf form as they are in human form. I knew, from firsthand experience, that this was not the case. I had seen tall, bulky men turn into werewolves that were almost scrawny by comparison and I had seen petite women become two-hundred- pound monsters. Despite the fact that Louis Chastel only stood a little over five and a half feet tall and was built like a jockey, his wolf was a two hundred plus pound beast.

As I had feared when I first saw the cabin, the massive picture window proved to be the weak point in the building's defenses. Chastel's wolf came through the glass in a single lunge that brought the whole window crashing into the great room, shards of glass flying in all directions. Amber and I both had the same reaction, flipping up over the back of the couch and allowing the furniture to take the flying glass rather than our bodies but neither of us escaped without some shallow cuts to face, arms and hands that were exposed when the Beast made his entrance.

I heard a low growl from Amber and turned to see her, golden- eyed with her face almost half shifted, pick up the heavy leather couch and throw it in Chastel's direction. The move seemed to surprise the werewolf; the couch actually hit him and, though he shrugged the heavy sofa off like rain, the flying piece of furniture did slow his assault.

I had no time to shift and I would have been hopelessly tangled in my clothes if I had tried. In my human form, the wolf had me at a huge disadvantage physically so I was going to have to use magic to even the odds. I opened my hand, scrawled the ice rune before me in vivid color, the energy of my soul's fire giving it power and sent the spell hard in Chastel's general direction. It did not have to hit him to be effective; it just had to get close enough to slow him down.

Chastel's wolf barked on a single low note, just as I would have done in dog form, and a shield of purple-black light manifested to take the brunt of the spell and diminish it. By the time it arrived, the magic barely frosted Chastel's coat but the distraction had given me precious moments to work up a second spell. It was imperative that I keep Chastel on the defensive since, if we engaged in magical combat in this enclosed space, the cabin was liable to come down on us.

I wanted to turn and search for Amber but I knew that my life and hers both depended on my attention. I feinted with a fire rune attack, forming a flashy fireball around my fist, and worked the earth rune, slinging the energy at the ground beneath Chastel's feet with my other hand. The wolf growled death at me as its feet stuck to the ground, mired in what felt like quicksand. I used a moment to turn and look for Amber but she was nowhere in sight.

The rogue werewolf growled and grunted several spells, trying to loosen the grip of the earth on his feet, as I rushed into the kitchen and seized my staff from the corner where I had propped it when we came in. The ash of the long walking stick felt good in my hands and, as soon as I picked up the piece, the runes along its length began to glow and the headpiece shone with a lambent silver glow. I pushed my will and the force of my Hel-born spirit into the staff and emerged from the kitchen to face the Beast.

Something resembling fear crept into the eyes of Chastel's

wolf as I walked slowly and carefully back into the room. I could see, from the way the muscles bunched under his coat, that he had worked out the counterspell for my earth rune and was prepared to leap at me once more. I pointed the staff at him and shouted the battle rune.

Chastel barely had time to bark his shield into place before the torrent of energy I had unleashed slammed into him, knocking him back several feet so that his back end stood on the deck outside the shattered window. My feet crunched on shards of glass as I moved steadily toward the wolf, worry for Amber niggling at the back of my mind.

"Chastel," I said, speaking in the Old French that he would most easily understand, "you cannot win this time. Even if you beat me, there are others to take up the hunt. You have given insult to one of the Lords of the Sidhe and he has sworn to me that he will call in the Wild Hunt if I cannot bring you in. Far better to give yourself up than face that."

I stood, waiting. I did not think Chastel would give up after so long a run but the Charter dictated that I had to at least attempt to bring him to justice

The Beast stood for a long moment, as though considering my words, and then threw back his head and emitted a sound that was suspiciously close to a laugh. That exposure of his throat was nearly his end.

I hadn't been able to see Amber because she had been up in the loft making her Change. When Chastel lifted his head to mock me, she launched herself over the railing of the loft, landed in a graceful roll, glass crunching off her fur and speared toward the larger wolf, her ears flat, fangs bared and hunting instincts fully engaged.

My lover's wolf didn't try for a frontal attack but moved obliquely, slashing with sharp fangs at Chastel's throat and a ripping a paw full of lethal claws across his shoulder and front leg, seeking to sever tendons and reduce the other wolf's ability to move. Chastel's wolf yelped in agony as claws opened his flesh and teeth opened his neck and Amber was away, into the darkness, before the other wolf had a chance to engage her.

The rogue werewolf limped into the great room and faced me. I could see that Amber had damaged his front leg severely but that the throat wound, although bloody, would not prove mortal. I backed a step at the low growl that emanated from Chastel, preparing myself for another assault but instead, he pivoted and, using his three good legs, propelled himself out into the forest, presumably in pursuit of the wolf that had injured him.

CHAPTER TWENTY-THREE

*D*espite the poor cell signal in the area, I managed to get a call to Al-lin. He cursed fervently, in several languages, when I revealed Chastel's strategy. We both should have seen it coming but there would be time for recriminations later; at present, we discussed strategies for a moment and decided on a course of action.

Right now, my prime objective was to go in pursuit of the rogue before he could catch up to Amber. I could use magic in both my forms but, if Chastel should run Amber to ground, he could commit all sorts of nastiness against her without ever touching her. She had been lucky with her surprise attack and Chastel was hobbled for a little while but his wounds would heal quickly and then she would be alone in the woods with an experienced hunter.

I stripped out of my clothes, careful of the glass on the floor, fastened a small device to a collar of stretchable lycra around my neck and changed to my hunting form. I stepped out into the cool night, the red light of my eyes reflecting eerily on the wooden rails of the deck, and raised my face in the slight breeze, letting loose a full-throated, bass howl, announcing to Louis Chastel that the hunter was about to become the hunted.

In the distance, a tenor voice responded in a beautiful ululating howl that let me know that my mate was alive and free . . . for the moment. I set my nose to the wind, crinkling it at Chastel's putrid scent and bounded between two birch trees into the High Peaks Wilderness.

In our conversations, I had learned that Amber knew how to navigate by GPS and that she could take a bearing on a map and follow it. I had explained to her that it was a little more difficult to navigate in wolf form unless you were following a scent and then back trailing yourself to get back. Amber was definitely not going to be following her back trail since she had to know that Chastel was not too far behind her but she also did not seem to be wandering aimlessly in the wilderness either. Her trail and Chastel's led almost due north, diverging slowly from Ampersand Lake's shoreline, and then curving slightly west toward the mountain of the same name.

I couldn't be sure of Amber's strategy—perhaps she reasoned that the mountainous terrain would slow the heavier wolf and give me a chance to catch up but the choice of that mountain had a hazard of which she might not be aware. The summit of this peak, at 3352 feet, was bare, denuded of trees by a settler named W.W. Ely in 1872 and kept that way by subsequent erosion and fires. If Amber maintained her present course and emerged into the open at the top of the mountain, she would be exposed to Chastel's line of sight and therefore his magic until she could get under cover again.

I rocketed through the thick deciduous growth, my huge, gaunt form stretched to the limits of its double suspended gallop, leaping downed trees and jagged boulders in my path. My inner senses told me that I was closing rapidly on the two wolves and that Amber still held a slight lead but we were approaching the mountaintop rapidly. I needed to do something to slow Chastel down but I was using every ounce of air I had to stay in the chase.

I dug deep into my own well of focus and concentration, setting my body on a sort of autopilot and bringing the image of Chastel's slavering wolf clearly into my mind. It was not enough to visualize in two dimensions, I had to make his image real and three dimensional, as though I were viewing him running directly in front of me.

Once I had the vision of Chastel's wolf clearly before me, I used a derivation of the earth rune spell that I had thrown at him earlier. This one was a bind rune. I reached into the core of fire that burned within my soul, charged the rune, and flung it at Chastel with an inarticulate snarl.

The result was immediate and gratifying. I was cresting the ridge of yet another foothill, rapidly approaching the base of Ampersand Mountain. In the valley between the two rises, deep in a lone copse of pine, I heard a muffled grunt and the sound of something heavy slamming into the soft cover of pine needles beneath the trees. As I plummeted down the hill toward the sound, I raised my voice once again and was gratified to hear Amber's bright, clear howl from about halfway up the side of the mountain. I marveled at her swiftness; she had managed to stay well ahead of her more experienced pursuer.

I turned my thoughts back to Chastel as I plunged into the deep shadows of the little valley and slowed. Rushing into a fight with a rogue werewolf was never a high percentage move and, with one as wily and experienced as the Beast, it would be outright suicidal. My keen ears detected no sound of movement from the little stand of pines and, as I approached, even though I was downwind, I caught no scent of the rogue. I slowed down to a slow-footed stalk, head held low and muscles bunched to spring if the need arose. The fiery flare of my eyes burned the forest a dim red as I approached the place where I had heard Chastel go down but, as I edged my way between the trunks of the trees, I became increasingly certain that the wolf was not there.

I came into a small clearing and placed my nose to the ground, watching carefully around me. The death-laden scent of my foe told me that Chastel had lain here not too long before. Where was he now?

Amber called, uncertain, in the distance but I could not afford to make an answering noise. From the sound of it, she was safely up the mountain, close to the place where the trees petered out onto the mountain's top.

I prowled the small clearing, unconsciously growling low in my throat with frustration before my own stupidity hit me. The slight tang of ozone in the air should have cued me. If a magic worker appears to have disappeared into thin air then, chances were, that individual had done just that. When he went down, Chastel knew that I would catch him unless he acted quickly. He had opened a Way and disappeared into that portal before I could bring him to ground. That meant that . . .

I was in motion before the thought even finished, giving full voice and willing Amber to come in my direction. She returned the call with alacrity, hearing the frantic tone, and I could discern that she was moving toward me at speed as I bounded recklessly up the side of the mountain, pulling from the fire at the core of my being, readying myself for a magic that I was ill prepared to use in my Dog form.

To my surprise, I felt the portal open above me, on the cleared mountaintop, rather than in immediate proximity to my fleeing mate, who was coming down the hill toward me at an amazing rate.

Laughter boomed down the side of the mountain, sharp and cynical. A voice, laden with the accents of old France and amplified to my ears by the power of magic, spoke to me. "You know, I could have dropped that portal right on top of her and spirited her away. That was not my intent."

I slowed to a stop, nearly a third of the way up the mountain and focused on my telepathic skill. "And what was your intent, Louis?" I asked, projecting to his mind.

The laughter again, soft, and sinister in the velvet darkness. "I just wanted you to know that I could have done it. That I can take what you value and that there is really nothing you can do about it."

I growled low to myself but strove to keep the exchange civil. "Perhaps. But now you are talking instead of fighting. You cannot keep running forever, Louis Chastel, and I have your scent now. Give yourself up."

"I will give myself up when they take my cold body from some wood, Black Dog, but before that happens, I am going to kill you."

My ears perked and, as I stood in the shadows of the tree canopy, I sensed Amber coming slowly up beside me. I was not certain that she could hear the exchange but she bumped her shoulder into me as she came near. I turned to nuzzle the fur of her ruff for a moment but then turned my mind back to the Beast. "Brave words, Louis, but you have not managed it yet."

"That is because I have not really been trying. I want your death to be a special one, hound."

I stiffened at the insult—hound is a werewolf pejorative term for the Black Dogs—but huffed away the tension before replying. "I understand why you would hate the Black Dogs, Louis, but it seems that your animosity to me is . . . something more."

Chastel almost hissed his venom as he replied, "Something more? How would you feel about a being that has been shaped and trained for one purpose: to kill you?"

I chuckled in his head, determined to keep him talking and, hopefully, off balance. "I am a Black Dog, Louis. I am born and bred to hunt rogue werewolves. You take too much importance to yourself."

I could almost hear the rogue shaking his head. "Foolish hound. Look at your own training versus that of the other Dogs.

Who else among your peers has been placed in harm's way so many times during training? Which Dog, besides you, has been allowed to train in magics other than the standards used by all Black Dogs."

It was my turn to shake my head. "I am sure that the Council had you in mind when they authorized my additional training, Louis, but most of the things I have learned, I have learned because I asked to learn them. I did it because I looked around me and could see that the rogues that we are tasked to bring in are becoming increasingly dangerous. I made the offer to take additional training and some forward thinkers on the Council decided that they could use me as a test case."

"Whether you're a happy accident or a planned missile to use against me," Chastel snarled, "I have to eliminate you and I have to do it in an open and spectacular way so that the Council knows that sending the Dogs against me is futile."

"Well then, what do you propose, Louis?"

Chastel cackled. "Black Dog, known in the human world as Zachary Collins, I hereby challenge you to the Duel Arcane, to take place on the ground of my choosing and at the time of my choosing."

My eyes lit fire red in my anger. "You what?! You have no legal standing for invoking the right of duel, Louis. I am a duly constituted Charter enforcement officer. You know what would happen if you chose to show your face on a dueling ground."

"If you choose the coward's way, Black Dog, then I will hunt you or, more importantly, I will hunt the woman. I will catch her and I will kill her and I will not even leave you her bones to weep over."

I paused for a moment, trying to work out why Chastel would make a groundless challenge. All I could conclude was that it was pure megalomania on his part or that, after years of being relentlessly hunted, his psyche had cracked under pressure.

After a moment's consideration, I replied, "Louis Chastel," I replied, in the formal words of answer, "you are an affront to sentient beings on both sides of the Veil. You threaten the innocent and your underhanded dealings show that you have no honor. Since you have been foolish enough to drop the gauntlet of challenge, I accept. Name the time and place where you will die, rogue."

CHAPTER TWENTY-FOUR

*C*hastel's gleeful chuckle echoed in my mind. "You will meet me on the clear ground at the top of this mountain at midnight tomorrow. You will bring no weapons but your magic."

"Seconds?" I asked

"Of course. Someone must witness your destruction. I would advise you to leave the girl at home. Once I have killed you, I might decide to take her as an additional prize. She is pleasant to look at."

Another voice popped in and suddenly, I knew that Amber had been listening the whole time. "I know one thing for certain, if he should lose, rest assured that if you try to take me I will tear your manhood from your body and feed it to you, even if it is with my dying breath."

Chastel positively giggled. "Oh, good, I like a woman with spirit."

My internal clock was ticking but, if I had been able to smile in my Dog form, I would have. This woman that the fates had mated me to was exceptional in many ways. Seeking to modulate my voice, I replied, "And what of the Hunt that Al-lin of the Greenwood has threatened to raise against you?"

Chastel's voice held a sneer as he replied, "The faery is an exile amongst his own people. He will go to his Lord and ask for the Hunt but there is no compelling reason for the People to call one, other than the insult I have paid to his personal honor. If he wants me, he will have to come for me himself and I will be ready to fight him with fire and cold iron."

I looked to the sky over the mountain and saw the blinking lights approaching rapidly. "Well, rogue, I think you are about to get your wish."

The device that I had hooked to my collar was a faery made derivation of the tracking devices that humans use for finding animals in the field. I had made certain to put it on before Changing and pursuing Chastel so that Al-lin would know exactly where to find me. I knew that, with his experienced troops, there was little chance that the Beast would go unnoticed on the bare mountaintop.

I was correct in my assumption. The strangely silent black helicopter hove to upon spotting the werewolf and a NightSun searchlight illuminated the bare rock, tracking something moving rapidly across the face of the mountaintop. My acute hearing brought me a strange huffing sound on the wind, like someone blowing out their cheeks repeatedly, but then I caught the sound of projectiles spanning off the solid marble top of the mountain. A dull whump followed and the sky above the mountain lit up with a brief and brilliant explosion, a shockingly white, phosphorescent light that seared the retinas and made me look away instantly. I heard and felt the chopper landing on the rock pad above.

I heard a click from the device and Al-lin's voice came to me as though he were standing next to me. "I do believe we put a bullet in that cur, Black Dog, and I have five teams on the ground looking for him. Stand by and we will give you a location if we need assistance." off.

I huffed loudly to acknowledge and the tiny transceiver clicked

Amber moved up tight against me and we stood like that for long moments, both listening to the sounds of the pursuit in the woods east of us. The humans were good but they could not possibly move as silently as a wolf or Black Dog in the forest. I could feel my mate shaking next to me and realized that she had to be starving after that run. I looked in her golden eyes and focused my thoughts. "You need food."

Amber raised expressive wolf eyebrows in a query and I responded, "Small game and stay close to me."

The red wolf bumped me with a well-muscled shoulder then turned and slipped quietly into the forest as I stood waiting, my own legs shaking with exhaustion from the long run. I heard the slow stalk of her foot pads and the sudden pounce followed by the death scream of a rabbit and my mouth watered involuntarily as I caught images of the kill and feeding from her lupine mind.

The transceiver clicked again and my ears perked as Al-lin's voice came through once more. "Sorry, Black Dog, lots of blood but no body. I am not sure what your situation is but I would suggest that you get to our base camp as soon as you can so that we can debrief and plot a strategy."

I woofed another acknowledgment and the transceiver clicked off once more.

Amber appeared in the clearing almost immediately, licking the last of the rabbit's blood from her chops. I stood for a moment, trying to get my priorities in order, but Amber beat me to it.

"You look done in, my dear," her voice said softly in my head, "I think we both need to feed thoroughly, then we need to go back, get some clothes and the Land Rover and meet your boss at his base camp. You need some rest since you have a duel to win tomorrow and neither of us would sleep securely in the cabin with that broken window."

I could only acquiesce to that logic so I motioned with my head for her to lead off.

Amber dropped her head and continued, "And I am taking the cost of that window out of his bank accounts after you have terminated that loathsome beast."

I couldn't form words in her mind so I simply opened to her and let her hear my laughter.

* * *

THREE AND A HALF HOURS LATER, Amber, Al-lin and I were sitting in a small shed at an abandoned airstrip that my employer had appropriated for a base. Al-lin was staring at me with a dropped jaw, something that one did not see often in a faery of any sort, particularly not one of the nobility.

"He did what?" Al-lin repeated, looking at me for confirmation.

Amber answered him, "Chastel issued a formal challenge to something called the Duel Arcane."

Al-lin turned to her, trying to close his mouth. "And you heard this how? The communication was telepathic, yes?"

Amber shrugged. "I am an untrained Oracle, according to all the people on your side I have met, and now I'm a werewolf. I don't know how I do some of the things I do," she shrugged eloquently, "I just do them."

Al-lin allowed himself a smile—he was a sucker for a pretty face—but then his countenance turned grim as he looked back to me. "And you accepted his Challenge, even though it had no merit? For gods' sake, why?"

"Think, Al-lin. I have studied Chastel and followed his career since my days in the Academy. He is acting completely out of character. This is an old wolf, one with a lot of experience evading capture and suddenly I run him to ground in less than a week? I am good but I am not that good. I expected to be hunting him up here for days, perhaps even weeks, but I find that he has left a trail that even a human could follow."

Al-lin surveyed me for a moment and then said quietly, "So, what do you think he is doing?"

"I think perhaps he has finally cracked from the strain of being hunted for so long. I can think of no other reason as to why he is behaving so erratically."

The elf lord gazed evenly at me. "There is always the possibility that someone else is pulling the strings."

I shook my head. "I think that's doubtful. Chastel is nothing if not arrogant. There is not much chance that anyone is going to talk him into acting against his interests and inclinations and almost zero chance that he could be compelled."

Al-lin pondered that for a moment and then nodded. "Just a thought, too much Faery politics in my youth. So, how do you feel about your chances in this duel?"

I shrugged. "We trained together, Al-lin, you know what I am capable of."

Al-lin pursed his lips and almost smiled. "I think it is good that this mountaintop is already denuded of plant life."

I nodded. "This is going to be a hell of a scrap. I am going to contact the Sigrun after I have slept and check to see if she knows of anyone that might have trained Chastel in our style of magic. I assume that you will act as my second?"

Al-lin tipped his head to the side. "Of course. I will be interested to see who Chastel brings as his second, if he brings one at all."

I raised my eyebrows. "So far, although his Challenge has no merit, he has abided by the rules. I suspect he will have a second. Most likely some reprobate he has Turned."

Amber leaned forward as I paused. "I know nothing about this duel thing other than that Chastel has already said he wants to take me as a prize," she made a face of disgust, "is there anything that I can do to feel useful in this mess?"

I shook my head. "I know this will not sit well but the Duel Arcane is conducted being to being. Any interference from outside is a forfeit and that is fatal since the magic that surrounds the field will turn on the one who is forfeit. The best thing you can do for me is to stay here, out of harm's way, and let me get this over with."

Amber nodded slowly, worry evident in her eyes. Then, she surprised Al-lin and I by rising, taking my arm, and looking at the elf lord, "Then, you will excuse me but I am putting this Black Dog to bed. I think that he is going to need some rest before this event tonight and I intend to see that he gets it."

Al-lin watched us depart for our makeshift lodgings in a large pavilion-style tent with a grin and a knowing look in his eye. I tried not to blush as my lover escorted me firmly from the room.

* * *

LEAVE it to a prince of the Sidhe to make sleeping in a pavilion tent a comfortable, almost sumptuous experience. The ground had been covered with old but very thick carpet in a vaguely Oriental style and the space had been equipped with a king-sized bed complete with green and gold comforters and matching, high thread count sheets. A bedside stand with a water jug, two glasses and a dish for more canid snouts rounded out the room.

I was so tired by the time Amber dragged me out of the meeting that it was all I could do to make use of the nearby facilities, trek to the tent, get the flaps dropped for some privacy and undress. Amber curled in warm and temptingly naked behind me but my fatigue was not going to let me act on what my body was thinking. I was asleep as soon as my head hit the pillow, wondering, even as I dropped into slumber, that I had not made my customary Change to Dog form for sleep.

CHAPTER TWENTY-FIVE

our hours later, I woke to the light of morning filtering under the tent flaps and, disentangling myself gently from my sleeping lover, rolled out of the comfortable bed, stretching, and Changing as I moved to the makeshift door and brushed the tent flap aside with my shoulder.

To their credit, Al-lin's men were unflappable. Most people, seeing a huge black hound with sullen, glowing red eyes emerge from a tent would either flee or, if they were bearing weapons, turn and fight. Instead, I was greeted with quiet good morning's and respectful nods as I padded through the camp. I was pleased to see that the perimeter guards were nicely alert at their stations, every twenty yards or so, around the rundown fence line and that they were heavily armed and wearing the latest ballistic armor. It was clear to me, as I made my way into the tree line, that I would have to be careful to show myself slowly and clearly as I came back to camp to avoid being fired on with automatic weapons or worse. I know a grenade launcher when I see one.

I was in no hurry; the day was still young and the duel was

not set until midnight. I strode quietly through the forest, hearing the light wind soughing in the branches, feeling the soft loam beneath my paw pads, scenting the rich and varied life of the wood as I looked for a small clearing I could use. Despite the night's exertion, I did not feel any the worse for wear and I wondered if Al-lin had not had one of his healers doing some quiet work as I slept.

Eventually, I wandered into a gap in the trees that would suit my purpose. The sun was just high enough to peak over the forest canopy so I lay down quietly in the soft grass of the meadow and cleared my mind. Many years ago, when I had graduated from the Sigrun's training, she had given me a particular sigil, her own sign, by which I might contact her should I have a need. I had only rarely used the sigil—her training had been very thorough and emphasized independence—but, on occasion, I had needed her greater expertise.

I focused on forming the sign before me, etching it in living flame and pouring a small amount of my soul's fire into it. When I felt the magic reach the right frequency, I Called, softly and respectfully, and then waited for a reply. I did not have to wait long; I felt the hard-edged vibration of the Sigrun's mind in mine almost immediately.

"Black Dog, are you well?" I was surprised to hear her voice edged with concern.

"Yes, Mother, I am fine. I simply needed some information from you, if you have a moment to speak."

"Ah, good. Sometimes, it is awkward living on this side of the Veil. One of the faery students here had word from one of his relatives that you and Al-lin of the Greenwood had been in a fight last night."

My Dog eyebrows rose. "Word travels fast. Yes, we had a bit of a set to with Chastel."

"If you are Calling me, then I assume that he survived?"

I nodded to myself. "Al-lin and his men did their best to put the werewolf down but he did escape. He was wounded but I have no doubt that he will be healed by the time I see him again."

I could almost see the query on her face. "It sounds as though you are expecting to see him soon?"

"Aye," I replied and gave her a concise account of the events of the evening.

When I had done there was silence for a moment. "He challenged you to the Duel Arcane? That is most unlike him and gives me pause."

I felt the stirrings of unease. "Why is that, Mother?"

I heard the Sigrun heave a sigh. "I have not followed the Beast's career as you have, Black Dog, but you know that the Beast has made it a part of his life's work to study every magic that he can."

"It is part of the reason that I chose to study with you, yes I wanted to work in a magical style that he and other rogues would not have easy access to."

"Alas, Black Dog, while much of what that animal has learned is rooted in the debased arts of the human wizards, I am sure that you are quite capable of countering him on that level. What worries me is a persistent rumor that I heard recently of a human who was ejected from training with the Gryms. You know how closed mouthed those old runesters are but I did manage to find out from their Old One, that this individual matched Chastel's description. The Old One would not tell why he was released but he did say that the person made it to the second level before he was deemed unfit for further training."

"Damn!" I exclaimed involuntarily, "So there is a good chance that he has had a thorough course in basic rune magic?"

"It would seem," the Sigrun said with evident disgust, "I would advise extreme caution in the duel, Black Dog. If Chastel can fend you off long enough to Summon one of the various nasty beings he has had luck with, you could be in serious difficulty."

"I thank you for the caution, Mother."

"You are most welcome. I know you, Zachary Collins, and I know that Louis Chastel may think he has learned the magic of the runes but he has not had the time to make it part of his flesh and bones as you have. Chastel may think he has given himself an edge. Let him be overconfident . . . right up 'til the moment, you lay him low."

My mouth dropped up in a tongue-lolling grin. My teacher did not often express such confidence in a pupil. "Thank you again for the warning, Mother, and I will remember what you have said."

"You do that. I expect to see you and Miss Morgan in my Hall soon. I owe you a feast." She signed off with an almost audible pop. I sighed and stretched myself out in the sun, feeling the tickle of the soft grass through my fur. The wind overhead had picked up and, as I looked to the sky, I noted cirrus clouds moving in from the north. It had been unseasonably warm for late October in the Adirondacks but I had a feeling that was about to end abruptly.

IN JUST THE short time since I had left the clearing, the temperature had fallen about five degrees and I wanted to check in with Al-lin and see what the forecast looked like for the night. The people of Faerie have the National Weather Service beat, hands down when it comes to climate prediction. Nothing was going to stop the duel that night but I wanted to know whether I would be fighting on a clear and cold night or amid a driving snowstorm.

AFTER SHOWING myself carefully to the guards and re-entering the camp, I crept quietly into my tent but the slight change in her breathing told me that Amber had awakened. My mate rolled up onto her elbow and patted the bed beside her. I thought for a moment about Changing but instead just hopped up onto the bed and settled my monstrous hound-self next to her. This was what I was, after all, in the deepest part of my being. I knew that my mate was deeply worried about my safety in the duel to come but it did not seem that words were going to allay her fears. Instead, I pushed back into her and offered the only comfort I could: my physical presence.

We lay that way for some time, the silence between us as meaningful as any words that we might say, until someone scratched at the flap of the tent. Amber pulled the covers over her and I jumped off the bed and made my way to stick my head out and see who called.

One of Al-lin's men, a rangy man in his thirties, stood at a respectful distance from the tent. "Sir, your presence is requested in the command . . . um, shed," he said in the clipped accent of someone with an upper-class British education. I wondered briefly what had brought him to Al-lin's service but simply nodded slowly to signify that I understood and the trooper set off toward the building himself. I turned back into the tent and was graced with the sight of my lover pulling a turquoise blue sweater over her head, shaking her red tresses out and smoothing the soft wool over her body in an unconscious gesture.

Amber was a beautiful woman in good physical condition when she became a werewolf; the changes in her body were already becoming evident. She was losing the little body fat she had been carrying and the definition of her abdominals was becoming more apparent. She turned to see me staring and smiled, holding a hand out to me. I approached slowly and shoulder bumped her in the thigh. She lost balance and sat heavily on the bed, chuckling as I placed my head on a hard belly, scooting her sweater up so that I could rest my snout on her. I sighed deeply and pulled my mind away from the warm fragrant flesh beneath my nose.

My mate scooted up on her elbows and regarded me for a moment. "No time, huh?"

I moved my head from side to side in the semblance of a head shake, my expression regretful, but she just smiled again. "Let's go see what Al-lin wants and then we are going to excuse ourselves, go for a run in the woods and find a nice quiet spot to . . . take the edge off, before this duel."

I backed away from her and Changed, moving to get my own clothes on. I could feel Amber's eyes on my naked body as I dressed and almost had an attack of modesty. I had been alone for so long that it was disconcerting to me to be regarded with undisguised lust. I shook the feeling off and resolved to enjoy my mate's regard as she had enjoyed mine.

When we were both dressed, Amber and I made the short walk to the makeshift command post. The faery prince looked grim when we walked through the door. "There you are. Good thing I sleep even less than a Black Dog, I have had information coming in from a number of sources. Most of it is not making me happy."

I listened as the wind picked up a notch outside. "Tell me about the weather first."

Al-lin nodded. "That is one of the things that I am not happy about. There is a very strong arctic cold front coming this way and it will hit before midnight. Conditions for the duel tonight are likely to be sub-optimal: blowing snow and limited visibility."

"So, I fight this one in a blizzard. It is not like the Sigrun never tested us in near zero visibility conditions."

"True, so I would say that your training gives you an advantage there."

I looked steadily at Al-lin. "I hear a but in there."

My boss looked down at some printouts in front of him. "The

weather is worrisome but we both know that it can be overcome and even used to your advantage. This is what is really worrying me." Al-lin handed me the top sheet off the pile of paper in front of him.

CHAPTER TWENTY-SIX

I took the report and scanned it quickly then handed it over to Amber. I looked directly at Al-lin. "Since when do you have access to the seers?"

Every faery court has at least one gifted seer whose sole job is to provide the leader of the court with information. In a non-magical setting, this individual would be an intelligence officer but rather than gathering intel from human and electronic sources, the seers of the faery courts rely on skills in remote viewing, spirit communication and prophecy to provide information to their lord or lady. Al-lin was an exile; he did not have access to those psychic resources.

Al-lin's face took on that blank look that said that he did not want to give too much away and my heart rate picked up involuntarily. "Son of a—! You have infiltrated someone into your father's court, haven't you?"

"It is better that you do not know the answer to that either way and you well know it, Black Dog."

I was tempted to push the point but knew that the terms of the elf's exile were a hot button for him and that pressing that button would provoke an unnecessary fight. I needed a good reliable second for this duel and choosing this time to poke my nose into faery politics was not going to endear me to him.

I made a conscious effort to relax my shoulders and stepped back from the table. "All I am going to say, as your friend, Al-lin, is to be very careful. I don't want you to end up with the Justiciars on your tail."

Al-lin bowed slightly. "Your concern is duly noted, Black Dog, and one that I share, believe me, but let us speak of the contents of this report."

Amber remained silent through our exchange but piped up now. "Someone want to explain this to me? It appears that the report is talking about the visions of some psychic. Zach, you said a seer. Is that anything like what I am going to end up doing?"

I saw Al-lin's attention sharpen and realized what an asset a fully trained Oracle would be to him. It occurred to me suddenly that I might be getting deeper into faery politics than I wanted. I filed that thought for future worry and turned my attention to Amber. "An Oracle is a very specific type of seer, attached, as you know, to one particular god form. Your training will be aligned to enhancing that communication with your Lady as well as working your overall psychic abilities. Suffice to say, that an Oracle can definitely provide intelligence like what you see here," I noted, pointing at the paper in her hand.

I glanced up at Al-lin who was watching me with an expression close to bemusement then continued, "This report appears to be something that came from the seer in Al-lin's father's court but, other than the very clear warning, I am not quite sure what to make of it. Al-lin, any thoughts on what this might mean?"

I swore that the faery lord turned a shade paler than his normal ivory complexion. "Oh, aye, I know exactly what it means. 'The Black Hag' that the seer keeps going on about is an ancient faery of the Unseelie Court. If you were a Christian, this would be the equivalent of someone pulling Beelzebub into the circle to deal with you. I have no idea how, in all the hells, this wolf found a way to Call her but the last time She was released, it required the powers of two major faery lords, both of whom almost died, to re-bind her. That fight set off the San Francisco earthquake of 1901. This time, she would be contained in a circle but . . ."

"She would squash the Black Dog flat just for being there."

Al-lin nodded somberly but I smiled. "Then my strategy is quite obvious. I must take him before he has a chance to attempt that invocation. I think that it is time that I acquainted him with the real magic of the runes."

I saw Amber start to ask questions but I stilled her with a glance. "I take back what I said earlier, I am going to need your assistance this evening."

* * *

THE DUEL ARCANE originated amongst human wizards. In their version of the duel, each of the combatant's steps into a circle that is then ritually sealed to prevent either of them from exiting until one of them wins the duel. Once the circle is sealed, each wizard calls forth a familiar and pours his or her magical might into that being as it fights the familiar of the other wizard.

The ritual of the duel arcane would be much the same for me. Some supernatural beings have familiars and fight in the wizard's way but shapeshifters actually become their familiars so a duel between shapeshifters was a test of combat magic. Given this fact, the circle we would fight in would be quite large but it would still be sealed by the fire of the earth and there would be no escape from it once it was raised.

Given what we had learned from Al-lin's source, Amber and I

did not have the luxury of stealing away to take the edge off. I contacted the Sigrun again and explained what we had learned and how I proposed to deal with the issue. Once she understood my strategy, the Mother of Runes was only too willing to help and Gated directly to the camp. Nonplussed by the tactical team that surrounded her or the deteriorating weather, my teacher took Amber in hand for some personal tutelage while I prepared myself for the duel.

Once Amber was securely squirreled away with the Sigrun, I consulted with Al-lin and he pointed out several places on the map where ley lines intersected. I could have just sensed my way into a ley intersection but did not want to waste the energy. I Changed and made my way to one of these spots, a ragged granite boulder jutting from a mountainside like a standing stone, where the earth's energy currents come closest to the surface and spent some time in meditation there, tapping into the earth's abundant energy, as the sky turned a slate blue-grey and the wind made me glad of my fur coat as the first snowflakes of the storm began to fall.

Once I had done, I hunted so that I was well fed and ready for my exertions of the night. I arrived back at the camp shaking snow from my coat as I stalked toward my quarters, intent on getting out of the increasing cold for a time. I have considerable resistance to the cold but I could not afford to let any factor, including hypothermia, effect my reflexes tonight.

The Sigrun was standing in the shadows, directly outside the tent and motioned for me to follow her before I could go in. Once we were well clear of the tent, the old runester turned to me and said quietly, "She has had a very intense day and I have left her to sleep until we must depart."

I woofed an acknowledgment and, not wanting to disturb my exhausted mate, turned aside to the deserted command hut. No one was there so I curled up in a dark spot in the corner and focused on my breathing until I slid into a fitful slumber.

* * *

I CAME to my feet instantly, wide awake as someone walked into my sleep space. Amber's smell washed over me a moment later and I relaxed as she dropped to her knees and threw her arms around my neck. "Hello, my Black Dog. Ready to do this?"

I huffed assent and she followed me, hand resting on my shoulder, as I made my way back to our makeshift quarters. I brushed the tent flap aside with my snout and stepped into my human form as I made my way to the footlocker that I had placed at the end of the bed.

Moving aside the top contents of the locker, I came to my ritual robe. I scribed the signs of my personal bind rune of power slowly and carefully over the robe, forming the sigil in my mind in crimson flame and then releasing the power into the cloth that would cover me in the battle to come. The bind rune burned deep into the woolen folds and I felt the spells that the Sigrun herself had woven into the cloth come to life.

I spoke the ritual prayer of invocation to Odin that all members of the Order used when going into combat, praying not for His assistance but simply for the strength to Become all that I could be in that night. With the staff the Sigrun had recently awarded me, the magical protections weaved into the very warp and weft of the robe I was wearing and the training of a more than one human lifetime in the magic of the North, I felt as ready for this battle as I could be.

I turned to Amber, who had been waiting quietly at the door of the tent, unconsciously keeping guard, and nodded my readiness.

Instead of moving back out into the gathering storm though, she stepped around to the side of the bed and opened one of her bags. Moving quickly, she divested herself of her civilian clothes and drew on a deep orange robe, trimmed in fox fur.

The blood-red runes that trimmed the sleeve were different

from the ones on mine and, as I tried to work out the meaning, my mate spoke again, "The Mother of Runes tells me that your sigils are for protection and combat. The ones on this robe are intended to help me with my communication with the Lady and . . . with any Others who might want to speak to me as I take the training. She said that normally this would have been given to me when I had completed the training but, given the circumstances, she felt I needed it tonight."

I nodded dumbly, momentarily taken by the expression on her lovely face. She looked at me curiously. "What?", she asked.

"I . . . you look marvelous in that color and the fox fur hood suits you."

Amber stroked the soft fur of the hood. "Normally, I would not wear real fur but . . . when she gives you something, you do not fuss." I laughed lightly. "Oh, no. Denying the Sigrun is not a high percentage move. We'd better get boots on before we both get frostbite and then find the others. My internal clock says we should be leaving soon."

Amber placed her hand on my arm to hold me for a moment as I turned to go. "Zach."

I kissed her quickly and my mate smiled at me and shook her head. "Apparently, everyone, including the Lady, is confident that I can do this thing. I guess I will just have to listen to them."

I smiled and stroked her hair back from her face. "Amber, I hate to tell you this but that is what being an Oracle is all about. Listening to and trusting the guidance you receive. "

She nodded quietly and placed her cheek against my chest for a moment. "So, the Mother told me today and believe me, I got the crash course but I am still afraid. I cannot let you down, Zach. I could not bear to lose you after all we've been through already."

I took her chin gently in hand and raised her eyes to mine. "We are in this together and we will get through it together. Now, let's get going before I say something stupid and over-emotional."

Amber smiled and shoulder bumped me, unconsciously emulating her wolf. We sat on the bed for a moment and pulled on warm socks and boots as we listened to the wind picking up outside the tent. Then, once we both had on appropriate foot-gear, I scooped up my staff and led the way out into the snow.

CHAPTER TWENTY-SEVEN

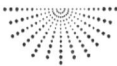

*A*l-lin had assured me that the weather would worsen as the night progressed and that, by morning, we would have well over a foot of snow but this duel was not going to go on all night. You did not place too magical heavyweights in a closed circle, remove all rules and expect that the fight was going to go on for hours. Most magical duels were settled in a matter of minutes. Even an epic duel, like the one between Al-lin and Ed-var of the clan Blacklake, had lasted less than an hour.

I focused on breathing deeply and relaxing as much as possible as Al-lin drove us to the meeting spot. As I had said before, Chastel seemed to be playing by the rules but this whole duel was entirely out of character for him. If he were to suddenly begin responding to his survival instincts, there had been very ample time for him to set an ambush and he certainly had the resources to pull one off, magical, or mundane.

Amber seemed to catch my unease and I felt her hand rest on my shoulder from the back seat as she, too, looked out into the thickening snow. I heard her take a deep whiff, as though she were scenting the air. "I may just be jumpy but it seems to me that there is something out there. I keep seeing flickers of motion out of the corner of my eye."

Al-lin raised the cryptozoological curiosity of my mate by responding simply, "They are wild fae, members of neither the Seelie or Unseelie Courts. I believe your people refer to them as Bigfoot but I detest that name; I tend to call them Sasquatch when I am speaking English."

Before Amber could really get into investigator mode, she had a chance to meet the object of her interest face to face. One of the Sasquatch stepped briefly out from behind a tree, making Amber gasp at its sheer size and bulk. The Sasquatch was easily eight feet tall, barrel-chested and covered with short dark fur. The being was a solid mass of muscle, so much so that it seemed to have no neck and its legs more closely resembled small tree trunks than ambulatory appendages. The huge male made a sign and faded back into the woods.

"All clear, according to our large friend," Al-lin noted, slowing the vehicle to a stop, "he has had the whole clan up here watching the area since I spoke with him yesterday. I doubt that we have anything to worry about."

I breathed a silent sigh of relief; no sign of an ambush meant one less thing to worry about. Al-lin turned to Amber and said, "This is where you get out, my dear. We do not want Chastel to know you are in the area. The Sasquatch will take you into the woods and keep watch over you as you play your part."

My mate looked leaned over the seat and kissed me quickly and then exited the vehicle. We watched her walk over to the tree line and waited until a much smaller female appeared and took her gently by the arm. Amber turned and waved and then vanished into the forest with her unusual escort.

* * *

AL-LIN PARKED the Hummer as far from the other vehicle in the car park as he could manage and we exited quickly, getting our first good look at Chastel and his second as we strode across the parking lot through blowing snow flurries to stand a couple of meters in front of them.

Chastel stood, robed in black with silver and dark purple thread tracing the sigils of his magic along the edges of his sleeves and around the hood which was thrown back to reveal his face. He was not a large man and, at first glance, most humans would probably not have viewed him as much of a threat. One attentive look at his face, though, with the dark eyes viewing everything around him as potential prey and the sharp teeth that never seemed to quite Change back to normal in his lean face, would put the lie to that first impression.

His companion was quite a lot taller than he, wearing, as was Al-lin, civilian clothes—boots, flannel lined jeans and a winter jacket with a deep hood that concealed his face. Chastel's second had the lithesome look and build of one of the faery but, without seeing his face, it was difficult to know much more. We would have to wait for the formal introductions.

Chastel started off snide. "Well, hound, I see you finally decided to show up. I thought perhaps you had decided to tuck your tail and run back to your precious Council."

Al-lin knew that I would be saving all my energy for the duel so he spoke instead. "We are five minutes before the appointed time, cur," he snarled. "I have personally advised that you be handed over to the Guild Warriors for even daring to issue this challenge. So, keep a civil tongue in your head, werewolf. It is not too late for me to issue the Call."

Chastel smiled. The long slow smile of a being that knows something you do not, or thinks he does. "Do you really, seriously, think that I would allow that, exile? The only reason that I have called you here is so that you can die. Both of you."

And that is when the night went, as the humans say, to hell in a handbasket.

* * *

SEVERAL THINGS HAPPENED ALL AT ONCE. The being standing next to Chastel disappeared into smoke and flickering flame. A Gate opened behind Chastel and he disappeared into it before either my employer or I could react. I wondered briefly where he was escaping to but then I heard a series of ululating calls in the distance. The Sasquatch, the bastard was going for Amber!

Before I even had a chance to fill with hot rage, the earth beneath my feet trembled. I looked wildly around me as the ground in several, evenly spaced places around the parking lot began to buckle and seemed to cave in on itself. Dark purple light tinged with silver, exactly like the embroidery on Chastel's robe, erupted from the sinkholes and noxious vapor rose to drift across the lot, stinking of Sulphur and decay. The temperature in the area seemed to rise by twenty degrees.

"Methinks," Al-lin noted dryly as he moved to place his back to mine, "that we are not going to like what will come out of those holes."

"Any chance of making a hasty retreat?" I asked.

Almost as if in response to my question, black smoke issued from the sinkhole closest to our vehicle, coalescing as it came into the semblance of giant horned ram with a serpent's body and six eyes that glowed with hellfire. The creature lowered its head and slammed it into the front of the Hummer, buckling the front end like an aluminum can and rendering the vehicle useless for anything resembling flight.

The monster turned to glare at us with glowing eyes, inky smoke pouring from all the sinkholes as it grew to tower over Al-lin and I. With contemptuous disregard, the monster turned once more for the truck and slamming its massive horns into the side as glass shattered out of all the windows and the tires exploded from the massive pressure placed on them.

There was light emanating from somewhere and I spared a glance to the forest around us. "Damn!" I cursed and Al-lin glanced up to see the shimmering lambent circle that surrounded the parking lot.

Chastel had obviously put a lot of work into this trap and, given the Sasquatch patrols recently, he had done it some time ago. Such forethought was one of his hallmarks but I could not imagine what his end game was as I grudgingly admired his magical snare. One circle was drawn inside the other and arcane symbols were carefully scripted, in the space between the two perimeters. I had studied enough grimoires to know that the circle was designed to invoke a specific presence and keep it in the confined space. If we moved to break the circle, we would be releasing the creature, obviously a demon of some sort, into Midlands. Not a good move and one that Chastel knew neither Al-lin nor I would risk.

The ram thing bellowed; the sound hitting us with an almost physical impact as the beast continued to maul the truck. If it kept scooting the vehicle across the lot, it was going to break the circle and run wild. I took stock of our situation and said quietly to Al-lin, "I am more prepared for a fight than you are. Think you can distract our monstrous friend there while I put together a serious invocation?"

Al-lin smiled wolfishly, "Of course. That Hellspawn is giving me a headache with all that bellowing and how am I going to explain the damaged truck to my insurance company? Seems I owe him a little something for my pain."

I knew that things were serious when my boss started quipping. "You know something, I don't?"

"Oh yes, Black Dog, congratulations. You are about to face Alamliel!"

I started. "The demon from the Greater Key, lord of a thousand legions of demons and so on?"

"The same, his specialty, bringing about the ruin of your enemies."

I stared at the ram thing with new respect. "Well, we better not let him out of this circle then. I expect there are lots of enemies to be ruined out there if he starts stomping around in the Midlands."

"My thoughts exactly, Black Dog. This might be a good time to see if Amber is safe and use her unique skills to aid you."

About that time, Alamliel seemed to remember that there was other, more interesting game in the circle with him, his attention moving to the smaller things in its circle. Al-lin paced slowly away from me, drawing his attention. "I give you greetings, demon. Neither of us wants to be here. There is no reason this has to come to blows."

A grating sound rumbled through the clearing and it took me a moment to recognize the sound as laughter. "Oh, but it does, elf lord," the demon replied in a voice that somehow resembled the buzzing warning of a rattlesnake, "you see, the werewolf and I have an agreement."

One of the sigils in the circle glowed more brightly. "By the inclusion of this sign," Alamliel continued, "I will be released into the world once I have ruined the two of you. It will be most . . . glorious to be free, even for a little while."

CHAPTER TWENTY-EIGHT

*S*ince a demon of the Greater Key is considered a major power and cannot simply be killed as a werewolf or lesser faery might, any mage faced with such a being has a choice in how to deal with the Fallen One. I made my choice as Al-lin barked the rune of fire and sent a gout of flame into the demon's face, leaping nimbly over a tail swipe that would have ended the fight if it had landed. I could not hear what rune Al-lin invoked next but assumed that it had to be one of the storm bringers since wind rose inside the circle and lashed Alamliel's eyes with ice and hail. Al-lin was not really hurting his opponent but he was doing a damned fine job of blinding the demon and keeping his attention focused away from me.

I had no intention of trying to duke it out with a demon. Al-lin had leveled a whole mountaintop when justly provoked and I could likely do the same but even power like that would not guarantee that we could defeat the monster. The old demons, the ones from the grimoires, are strong and they have powerful defenses. Sending the Fallen One back to his home was an attractive proposition but required that you know where to send the devil. There is more than one hell and returning the demon to the wrong place would cause a major incident in the Underworld. That left me with the choice of calling for major backup.

I folded my hands into the sleeves of my robe and ducked my head in concentration.

I began simply, with the rune of protection, Algiz, also called Elhaz, or the elk. The figure of the rune is a straight line with two lines branching off at forty-five-degree angles.

I opened my eyes to see the rune, limned in flickering rainbow light, drawing its energy from Bifrost, the Rainbow Bridge, hanging before me. The atmosphere around me had shifted and I noted, in the periphery of my consciousness, the attention of the demon turning to me. I shut this out of my mind, forming a single Name on my lips and vibrating it out into the ether, the runes of my staff and its headpiece glowing softly as the power thrummed forth across the Planes seeking the Being I had called.

For long moments, I waited and despair had begun to gnaw at the back of my mind, eroding my concentration. I was aware that the demon had connected with one of his tail swipes and knocked Al-lin halfway across the circle, dangerously close to where I stood. I was conscious of the six glowing red eyes bearing down on me and my fallen comrade, of my heart rate beginning to pick up despite my near trance state and of Al-lin climbing slowly to his feet, seeking within for another spell.

And then I heard the sound I had been longing for.

Different magicians have described it in different ways. Some say that it sounds like the tolling of a church bell high in a tower, others that it vibrates through them like a tuning fork struck to just the right resonance, still others that it is like the sound of a mighty rushing wind. I guess that it simply depends on the attainment of the magician.

For me, the sound was smaller than I expected, not a great gong or hurricane wind but a chime struck lightly. The effect though was instantaneous and unmistakable. Peace poured through me like the cool water of a mountain stream slaking my thirst. The runes on my staff lit with white radiance almost too bright to look at and a Voice spoke calmly. It was only later that I realized that the Voice was coming through my vocal cords.

"Alamliel!" the Voice said. The words were not loud but they would have commanded the attention of any but the higher gods.

The demon froze, its six eyes swiveling to stare at me, or rather That which occupied my space. Some part of me could almost smell the brimstone as the Fallen One turned to face this new adversary. "What have I to do with thee, Azrael?"

I am a Black Dog. My people have been associated with death since humans began telling tales. I figured that, if I were going to try to invoke an archangel, it should be one with whom I have a better acquaintance. It seemed that my gambit had worked.

Azrael turned my body to face the demon more directly and spoke once more. "You know why I am here, Fallen One. This being's memories tell me that you have been called into this circle by a sorcerer and have been promised release if you meet his conditions. Specifically, that you are to slay the Sidhe and the Black Dog trapped in this construct with you. You should have known," the Voice continued with something akin to chiding, "that we would not tolerate your manifested presence for long here in the realm of humans."

Alamliel drew himself up straight and had the temerity to laugh in the Archangel's face. "Ah, but it would have been glorious while it lasted. I am sure the Prince of the Hosts would have responded to the urgent prayers of Yahweh's servants and bound me back but it was worth it to me to have a short time to do as I wished. So many I could have ruined before the shackles fell on me once more . . ."

My physical body did not even see the ram-headed serpent move. The strike came that fast. Apparently, though, Azrael was used to dealing with the perfidy of demons. One moment, I was standing on the far side of the parking lot, facing Alamliel and the next, I was standing behind the demon as his horns slammed into the place I had been standing a moment before.

"Surely, Alamliel," the Archangel chided, "you did not think that would work. I am quite capable of surviving without this physical body and more than capable of sending you back where you belong."

"Then why not let this thing that is not human die. That is what you do, isn't it?" the demon taunted.

Azrael sighed, the benighted sound of a teacher trying to get through to a particularly dense pupil. "You know quite well what I do, demon. It is not time for this one to depart. Now, are you going to continue this childish display and force me to banish you or will you go your way in peace?"

Alamliel seemed to consider for a moment and the part of me that felt mashed flat against the back of my skull began to hope that the Fallen One would depart without any more fighting. Azrael, however, was not fooled by the demon's seeming contemplation of his options. I felt a twitch of power that I could not identify until the demon's eyes flared into harsh red flame and it opened its mouth and spewed forth a jet of purple-black flame. The angel in me lifted my hand and radiance spilled forth, forming into a half dome shield that protected my body. A smaller shield sprang to life around Al-lin who had wisely crept into a spot as far as he could get from the two combatants.

In the brief moment of distraction, he had created, Alamliel made his real move. Using all his supernatural speed, the demon turned and slammed his head into the demolished Hummer, shoving the heavy vehicle across the lines of both circles and breaking the magical snare. The magical construct collapsed with an audible snap and ear popping change of pressure and I thought I heard the archangel murmur something like, "Oh hell", he said as he blurred into motion after the quickly escaping demon.

Despite his unnatural speed, Alamliel was not going to outrun me in the forest, much less me plus an Archangel. My hands seized the tail of the serpent before it had gone a hundred yards and pulled it to a firm stop. The devil turned on Azrael, seeking once more to smash me into the ground like a tent peg, but my angelic invitee stopped the crushing head on my upraised palm, grabbed the horns and twisted, for all the world like some Western cowboy wrestling a recalcitrant calf. Alamliel wound up on his back, thrashing as the angel struggled to hold him while preparing the power to send him back.

Al-lin chose that moment to remind everyone that he was a prince of the Daoine Sidhe. I heard his voice ring in clarion brilliance through the wood, speaking a short phrase in his flowing native tongue and the forest came to life around us. Vines and tendrils sprang from the ground and wound their way through the offending horns, replacing themselves as often as they were broken, as the roots of trees in the area grew with supernatural swiftness, snaking up to loop around the curl of the twisting rack and add their strength to the binding. Within seconds, Alamliel's head was effectively pinned to the ground by an overgrowing tangle of forest vegetation which was beginning to spiral down and cover the upper part of the snake torso.

Azrael watched the proceedings with some amusement and then, once he was certain the demon was fairly secure, released the horns and looked down at his adversary. Alamliel was struggling against his bonds and given enough time, he might have wriggled loose but the Archangel had no intention of giving him that time. I felt the unfamiliar power gather around me as radiance began to fill the space between the trees where we stood. Something which looked like a Gate, only much, much larger, opened before us and then turned into a spinning vortex. The Archangel of Death spoke a Word in a Voice that sounded once more, to me, like the tinkling of chimes.

Alamliel howled an ancient curse even as his manifested body seemed to fly apart and be sucked into the whirling vortex of energy. It was over in a moment and silence descended so swiftly that I could still hear the ringing in my ears from Alamliel's howling exit.

Azrael was still standing inside me when Al-lin limped up to us. The angel spoke softly in the hush that followed our combat. "Well met, Al-lin of the Greenwood. I offer thanks for your assistance this night."

Al-lin raised his chin slightly, obviously exhausted. "You would have defeated the demon one way or the other, Shining One, I simply hastened the process a little."

Azrael used my form to nod. "True, but you shortened the time it took to return the devil to his place. I admit that I was quite surprised to receive this Call from one who does not normally operate in our planes. The Black Dog will require some care and healing after this exertion. Get him back to your camp and I will send ministers to him that will have him on his feet before the moon rises tomorrow. I must go before I tax this one's body beyond even our ability to heal."

Al-lin opened his mouth to say more but then closed it and simply nodded. I felt a brief tugging sensation at the top of my head, then a wave of dizziness followed swiftly by darkness.

CHAPTER TWENTY-NINE

I was trying to drag myself to consciousness, aware, for some time, only of radiant light and the soft chime that I had come to recognize as angelic voices. Part of me wanted to bask in the glow of that radiance, lose myself in its healing depths and stay there until my battered body signaled that it was repaired and ready for action.

It was not that I had taken any physical damage in the conflict with the demon. I had not. What I had done though, invoking the Archangel of Death into my corporeal form, was roughly equivalent to running a 220-volt current through a wiring system that was only designed for 120 volts. My energetic system was cooked which meant that, unless I healed thoroughly, I was not going to have full use of my magic.

That logical part of me, that said that I should allow the Shining Ones to complete their work, was at war with my emotional side. When I had lost consciousness, Amber had still been in critical danger and Chastel, damn his black soul, was still on the loose. Even if Amber had been out of the picture completely, I would have been fighting the angels; my sense of duty was over-developed and I could not allow Chastel to run free for one minute longer than was necessary.

I was distantly aware of tossing in my sleep, trying to come back to consciousness, when I felt a soft cool hand on my brow and heard Amber's voice. "Shhh, love. Lie still. I'm alright."

I felt as though I were suspended in cotton but my face must have shown the question in my mind. Al-lin's voice spoke on the other side of the bed where I lay. "You owe the Sasquatch a great debt. Apparently, when Chastel came for your mate, they spirited her into the forest, keeping her away from him at great cost to their people. They lost two males of the clan and two others are under the care of my healers. Chastel would likely have continued the pursuit had not one of their shamans opened a Way and escaped to the Other Side with her briefly. Now, devil dog, the best thing you can do is sleep. The Shining One promised us that you would be fit for action by the time the moon rises tonight."

Despite the fae lord's words, I wanted to get back into the hunt but something laid an ethereal hand on my head again and spoke a word in the dialect of the angels. Whatever the Word was, it sent me back into sleep.

* * *

I WOKE SOMETIME LATER, alone. I stretched my human form carefully, to see that all my parts were in working order. I threw the covers back slowly, still testing my body's strength, and dropped my feet over the edge of the bed, preparing to stand. Getting vertical caused some brief vertigo but the spinning passed quickly and I stood cautiously.

My legs seemed to work once I got onto two feet and I wondered if I dared Change to see how my true self was feeling. My stomach chose that moment to practically roar and I realized part of the reason I was still feeling weak and shaky. I had used an enormous amount of energy the night before and had not had a chance to replenish my body's stores. I needed to eat . . . now.

I opened the footlocker and removed some sweats, a t-shirt and a heavy down jacket against the cold I knew I would face once I exited the tent. My nose told me that the snow had continued to fall; I could pick up the cold crispness of the ice crystals even in my weakened state.

Once I had clothing on and boots laced, I pushed past the flap of the tent and almost tripped over the Sigrun in the twilit gloaming. The older woman was kneeling in the snow, as though she did such things all the time, stationed directly outside the door of the tent, and had, evidently, been meditating when I came barging out in search of sustenance.

She came to her feet with an ease that belied her years and bestowed me with a rare smile from beneath her hooded cloak. "Black Dog, it is good to see you moving again. It is not often that one of our Order does battle with a demon and it is even rarer that he uses an angelic invocation to defeat his foe. Your feat will be sung of by the fires of our Hall for some time to come."

I bowed carefully. "I owe my life to your training, lady. The angelic bit was a touch of inspired madness. I had no idea that the Archangel would actually choose to manifest in me."

The Sigrun regarded me with humor dancing in her eyes. "When such Beings respond to a Call, my student, they go where they choose. You did well to come out of that combat as well as you did."

My stomach roared once more and the Sigrun chuckled. "Come, Black Dog, we have meat prepared and laid out for you. I knew that you would be famished when you rose."

I wanted to go to the command center and see where things stood but, when I expressed that desire, the Sigrun only cast her eyes sideways at me and kept walking. I knew better than to argue with my old teacher so I followed her quietly across the compound, wading through a little over a foot of snow, and into what I took to be a mess tent. True to her word, several cuts of choice meat, uncooked and still bloody, lay on a platter, on the main table as we entered. The security detail had eaten in shifts long before we arrived so the Sigrun and I were alone as I shifted my jaw structure and set to work on the steaks.

By the time I had completed my repast, Amber and Al-lin had appeared and seated themselves at the table with myself and my teacher. All of them had seen me eat before so I felt no self-consciousness but I noted that my lover seemed very subdued, even as she sat and watched me with relief in her eyes.

I finished my meal and carried the platter back into the kitchen area. Everyone watched me in silence until I returned to the table. "I guess you're all looking for a status report so I will tell you that I feel pretty fit. Still, a little stiff and I have not tried to Change yet but, considering what happened last night, I seem to have come through the experience with minimal damage."

I looked at my lover with questioning eyes. She seemed to flinch inwardly but returned my gaze after a moment. "It's difficult for me to talk about what happened last night. It was horrible and, if the Sasquatch hadn't been there, that monster would have gotten me. I didn't even have time to Change and try to defend myself. That sick, twisted old wolf hunted me and some of my defenders died to keep me from him. There is one response we can make to that suffering. We have to bring that animal in—dead or alive—and honestly, I would have no qualms about standing over his cooling corpse right now."

I nodded slowly, struggling with my own feelings. "And that is exactly what Chastel wants. He wants us to strike out at him in rage just like a good fighter wants his opponent to swing in anger. Your instincts want blood and your human nature wants vengeance but we have to keep our heads, develop a sound strategy and implement it."

Amber stared at me for a moment, green eyes intense, her

anger an almost palpable force on my skin. "How can you be so cool?" she asked in a voice just short of icy.

I returned the challenging stare calmly, reminding myself that she was a new wolf and that this was the first time she had really had cause for calculated enmity since her Change. She was struggling not only with very human emotion but with the instincts of an apex predator that felt threatened in its territory. After a moment, my mate realized that her open-eyed stare was a challenge and dropped her eyes with a heavy sigh. "So, this is one of those testing times you warned me about, huh?"

I reached across the table and took her hand carefully in mine. "And the fact that you are asking tells me that you passed."

My lover lifted a shoulder in a shrug, her movements still tight with suppressed animosity. "I am not sure I have won this battle but at least I see your point. I guess that is something."

The Sigrun chose that moment to interject. "It is more than something, child. I have seen that you can control yourself—both in your training and, now when the worst has befallen you. Hold your head up, daughter of Morgan, you are doing far better than many wolves who have been Changed for years."

Amber took her hand from mine and brushed the hair out of her face, taking a deep breath and letting it all the way out before responding, "I don't feel very in control but I will take the word of the experts." She looked to Al-lin and he picked up the conversation seamlessly.

"While you were basking in angelic healing, we have been busy. The local fey are in an uproar after all the dark magic flung around in the forest last night and have been coming forward of their own accord to report Chastel."

My ears pricked up, even in my human form, which must have looked odd. I turned to Al-lin. "You know where he is then?"

"I do not have exact map coordinates but several different reports put him back in the vicinity of that house we investigated. I had Edward take all the reports we received, both mundane and otherwise, grid them out and attempt to triangulate a position. He found what he calls a cluster of reports in the area around the house where we were first going to flush Chastel into the open."

The elf lord continued, "There is a little-known cavern in the area, imaginatively named Thompson's Hole. Nothing to excite the local cavers but it would be a perfect place for Chastel to hole up."

The Sigrun and I exchanged glances. "I agree that it is worth checking out but a cave, with its access to the chthonic energies is a perfect place to spring something nasty. We need a good magical recon of the area."

Al-lin and the Sigrun nodded almost simultaneously. After a moment, Al-lin spoke, "The Shining One said that you would be ready to move out by moon rise tonight but you still look a little pale to me. I will handle the survey of the area; you need to rest more before going after this rogue, I think."

I wanted to argue with him but, given how my body still felt, I knew that it would be pointless and simply a matter of being stubborn. Already, fatigue weighed heavily on me again and I could see, by the slight circles under her eyes, that Amber needed sleep as well. Gods only knew how long she had sat up with me the night before. I suppressed my impatience and rose, taking Amber by the hand as I did and heading back to our tent.

We were both asleep within moments of crawling into bed.

CHAPTER THIRTY

*J*woke in the darkness to an eerie, ululating howling throughout the camp, something between a wolf's cry and the primal scream of a human in agony. I rolled from the bed and into my dog form in a single motion born of long practice and heard Amber wake and begin her Change as I stormed through the flap of the tent, all senses alert for danger. The snow was trampled into paths throughout the camp and I followed one silently, pulling from the fire that burned within me and unconsciously seeking for any stray ley lines or other sources of energy that I might need if we needed to combat magic with magic. After the perfidy of the night before, I was spoiling for a straight up fight.

I rounded one of the tents that had been set up to house the security forces and came into the clearing where the airstrip had once been. I saw Al-lin standing a few meters away and was surprised when Amber's rangy wolf sprinted up to stand beside me. It seemed that her Change was getting quicker every time she made the transition. Although Al-lin's team had not set up full, glaring perimeter lighting, her golden eyes shone brightly in the soft light coming from a few lamps scattered through the camp as we stalked out to join my employer on the airstrip.

Al-lin was standing, facing out toward the dark forest, a quizzical expression on his face. He waved a calm greeting as Amber and I joined him and motioned for silence. I did not see the Sigrun; I assumed that she had returned to her hall. We were on our own.

After pausing for a moment, Al-lin cupped his hands to his mouth and produced a howl that sounded remarkably like the one that had emanated from the forest. Then, he made a hand signal and I saw the trooper who had been watching him with binoculars from the perimeter speak into a radio transceiver. All the security forces went to port arms, still alert but not on immediate alert for hostilities. I dropped my ears back and muttered a low querying sound at Al-lin.

Al-lin glanced down at me and gestured toward the perimeter fencing. I looked off at the point that he indicated and saw a huge male Sasquatch ease out of cover and approach the fence. One of the unflappable perimeter guardians moved to a nearby gate, produced a key from his pocket, unlocked a padlock and unwound the chain securing the gate. Two more men from the detail joined him to watch the gate as the Sasquatch eased through, ducking his head to make his way through the mere eight-foot portal.

The big male was obviously uncomfortable out in the open but approached Al-lin with alacrity.

I had never been this close to a Sasquatch before; they are an elusive tribe of the fey and they tend to fade into the forest or disappear through Gates unless they have business with you or are accidentally caught in the open. This male was a fine example of the species though, somewhere over nine feet tall, covered in coarse brownish red hair except for the soles of his feet and the palms of his hands. The hair around his neck and intelligent, wide-eyed face grew longer, almost giving the appearance of a mane draping his shoulders.

Al-lin made a little bow to the Sasquatch and the creature returned the gesture with ponderous grace. The elf lord then listened carefully and seemed to understand as the Sasquatch emitted a series of clicks, whistles, moans, and growls coupled with the occasional clacking of its teeth. There was no real way that my friend could reply but he made himself understood through the use of an intricate sign language that involved a complex weaving of the fingers.

After several interchanges, Al-lin turned to Amber and me and spoke. "Seems that we are being offered some unexpected assistance. The Sasquatch held a tribal council last night, after the initial mourning for their fallen, and decided that they needed to take a more active role in removing this threat from their forest. What say you, Black Dog?"

I considered for a moment, then focused my energy to speak quietly to Al-lin's mind. "This is the tribal chieftain?"

Al-lin nodded and added, "The matriarch of their clan has given her blessing as well."

"Tell the chieftain that we mourn the loss of his warriors with him. You may tell him, too, that I have personally vowed to take this rogue in, and that if I am unable to do this, my own clan will not rest until this werewolf is in custody or dead. We would be honored to accept his tribe's aid. Please, ask him if his people would be willing to survey the area that we talked about earlier and let us know exactly what we face."

Al-lin nodded then translated what I had said into the flowing sign language that he had been using. The Sasquatch replied with a small roar and a series of tooth clacks, followed by a chuffing sound that seemed to me to be interrogative.

Al-lin suppressed a smile and turned back to me. "He says that his tribe would be honored to do the advance scouting but asks if there is something more they can do to help us. His language, in reference to your rogue, was quite colorful."

I thought for a moment and then voiced an idea to Al-lin. I swear that the elf is part shifter; his smile, as he turned back to the Sasquatch leader and relayed my request, was positively wolfish. The chieftain regarded me with something approaching humor in his eyes as he chattered a short reply.

Al-lin nodded and turned back to me. "He says that they would be most happy to set that up for you. The dawn approaches, he must return to his tribe and begin the reconnoiter of the area. The tribe will report back once they have information for us."

I bowed my dog form's head to the chieftain. "Please thank the chief for me, Al-lin, and let him know that we look forward to seeing him soon."

Al-lin relayed my message and then looked to the guards at the gate. The Sasquatch chieftain approached them slowly and then exited once the gate was open, disappearing into the forest with remarkable ease for a being of that size.

* * *

AMBER WAS NOT happy about involving the people of the forest further but understood that they needed to remove the plague from their woods and that we could not afford to be picky about assistance. She also understood that I was doing all I could to keep the Sasquatch out of the line of fire.

Once that was settled, both our thoughts turned longingly to the wildwood beyond the fence.

The sun would be coming up soon and there was no reason not to get some wilderness time in now that the Sasquatch clan was handling our advanced scouting. I looked to Al-lin, who made a shooing gesture with his hand, and then I moved toward the gate, my mate following at my shoulder.

Amber and I returned to the makeshift camp around midday and, after the customary cautious exit from the woods, were admitted back into the compound. We had run hard and fed well so we made our way straight back to our tent, jumped onto the bed and folded over each other for a much-needed nap.

I, of course, woke first. Amber was still adjusting to the energetic strains of being a lycanthrope and, even though her adjustment to her new condition had been remarkable, she still required more rest than normal. I untangled myself from her slowly, so as not to disturb her, and rolled over the side of the bed and into my human form.

I started to dress, as silently as I could, and was startled when a human hand reached out to stroke my bare flank. I swung around to see my mate in her very inviting human form, looking at me with eyes that left no question about what she had in mind. I was all too willing to rejoin her in the big bed.

Afterward, as we lay together in a warm embrace, my mate smiled and kissed me lightly, noting my wandering eyes. "You are ogling me, my dog."

I smiled and tried not to make it too lascivious. "Indeed, I am, my wolf. I know that you have not been with anyone in quite some time but, for me, it has literally been decades."

Amber looked shocked. "There's been no one else in that long. Not even . . . um, flings?"

I shook my head. "Not since the last world war. I had an affair with a lone wolf while I was in Europe; she was working with the Resistance on the mainland and I was investigating reports that the Nazis were deliberately making werewolves to enhance their army."

Amber laid her hand gently on my chest and I realized that the old sorrow must be showing on my face. "You don't have to talk about this if you don't want to. I did not want to open an old wound." I shook my head. "No, it is better that you know. It will help you understand when I seem over-protective of you."

My mate subsided a little but I noticed that she was holding me a little closer. I took a deep breath and continued. "Her name was, I do not joke, Jane but she was anything but plain. She looked nothing like you, much shorter, blonde, brilliant blue eyes when she was in her human form. I happened to be coming into a little berg in Southern Germany when her group was coming out after a small sabotage mission. They were ambushed by a team of SS commandos and I showed up in time to scare the Nazis right out of their foxholes."

"Afterward, I chose to travel with her unit since it seemed the best way to fulfill my own mission. One thing led to another and we became lovers."

Amber's brow creased in that way she had when she was considering something. "But there was no mate bond?"

I shook my head. "No, we enjoyed each other and ran together. I did love her in a human sort of way, I guess, but nothing like what we have."

"Judging from the expression on your face earlier, this did not end well. She died?"

I nodded, a hard lump in my throat. "As it turned out, the Nazis, along with their experiments in dark magic of varying sorts, had actually managed to find a real werewolf and were using the poor bastard to infect some of their soldiers. Three of those soldiers, fanatical SS types, actually made it through the Change with their minds intact and formed a pack that specialized in hunting down the resistance."

Horror crept across Amber's face. "And they caught up to your Jane?"

I bobbed my head in agreement. "I hunted those wolves into the Bavarian Mountains and I did not offer them the chance to surrender. I terminated their miserable existences, swiftly and without mercy. Then I tracked down the captured werewolf that the Nazis were using to infect people but ended up releasing him. He was a victim, not a bad guy and we are friends to this day."

I could see unshed tears brimming in my lover's eyes. "No wonder there have been no others until now. Even if she had only been a close friend . . ."

All I could do was nod again and tuck myself in close to my lover's side.

CHAPTER THIRTY-ONE

*E*ventually, I threw back the covers and rolled down to the end of the bed, rooting around in the chest until I found the box I was looking for. I sat back up in bed next to Amber and presented her with the small, ornately carved wooden cask. "I wanted to give you something as a token of our mate bond and this seems a particularly appropriate time."

Amber took the box curiously, examining the ornate Celtic lacework carved into it before opening it. She gasped at the contents and then looked at me. "I do not recognize the stone. Something from the Other Side?"

I nodded. "The faery tribes have an unpronounceable name for them but you can translate it as fire gems—something like the opal, only the intrinsic energy in the stone makes it glow if you put a little will into it. The chain is elven silver. You do not have to worry about shifting in it; it is enchanted and will always be just the right size and is virtually unbreakable. I've had this piece for a few years. It was given to me by one of the Tuatha after I assisted Al-lin in the recovery of her child. She told me to keep it for someone who was beloved to me and I could not think of a more fitting gift to give you."

My lover turned and allowed me to fasten the almost invisible chain around her neck. There was a slight tingle of power as the chain adjusted to its wearer. When I looked the jewel was hanging just below the hollow of her throat, perfectly positioned so that it would not be in her way but not so closely held that the chain became a choker.

I started to instruct her in how to make the stone light up but, at that precise moment, the ululating call of the Sasquatch chieftain broke over the camp and, once again, all hell broke loose.

* * *

I ROLLED from the bed and into my Black Dog form instinctively even as the sound of sporadic gunfire broke out along the camp's perimeter. A chill shot through me as a wolf howled and I thought for a moment that Chastel was making an assault on the camp himself but then another howl broke out, coming from the opposite direction, followed by a chorus of barks, yaps and the peculiar wolf sound that resembles an attempt at grumbling speech. I heard at least six distinct voices in that pack of werewolves and it dawned on me what Chastel had been doing with at least some of the hikers and others who had disappeared over the last month.

The rogue had been creating a little army to fight me. Six werewolves would be more than enough to distract me as Chastel readied whatever new horror he was about to unleash on us.

As I came out through the little tent city and into the clear space of the landing strip, I saw that the situation was worse than I thought. Somehow, the wolves had breached the perimeter fence and four of them were already inside. The security teams had obviously been briefed on how to handle this type of threat; they had broken into groups of three, formed up back-to-back and were firing short, controlled bursts at the rapidly moving wolves. Chances of a hit, given the werewolf's supernatural speed, were minimal but, as long as their ammo held, they could keep the wolves from approaching too closely.

I didn't have time for subtlety and there was no reason to expect that these wolves were going to come in quietly. Chastel knew his business and he would have recruited only those who lusted after the power of being a werewolf. He had had time to subvert them thoroughly and there was only one thing I could give them now...a clean death.

I boomed a challenging howl of my own, shaded with the power of death that follows me so closely in my Black Dog form, and arrowed across the airstrip at the wolf nearest me. This one was a large gray and he turned as I approached, coming to meet me in his madness, barking a warning to his pack. A savage growl sounded off my flank and I thought for a moment that I was being ambushed until I saw Amber's lithe red wolf rocket out in front of me and slam into the rogue, taking him neatly under his center of balance and knocking him onto his back.

The wolf didn't even have time to cry out before I took his throat out in one savage jerk, ensuring that he would not rise from the snow again. The blood loss would kill him before he could regenerate.

Amber's wolf had barely broken stride after taking the rogue off his feet and she was already fast approaching a second wolf that had come in answer to his pack mate's warning. I could tell by a subtle adjustment in the way she held her tail that Amber knew she had lost the element of surprise. She ran straight at the new threat, a gray but with lots of brown in his coat, then broke right as the other werewolf gathered itself to spring on her.

The brown tinted wolf missed his leap entirely and Amber skidded on four paws in the snow, pulling hard to come in behind the rogue. Before her opponent could recover, she had ripped vicious fangs through the tendons in the backs of his legs, hamstringing him. Even a werewolf can only heal so fast and the rogue had no chance to recover before I loomed up. I did what I had to do, picking the wolf up in massive jaws and shaking him until his spine snapped. The limp form that dropped from my mouth would not rise again.

Two of the wolves that had penetrated the perimeter were circling one of the security triads at the end of the airstrip, dodging and jinking to avoid the gunfire aimed at them, but I could not detect the other two. As Amber and I came like swift death down the strip, Al-lin stepped into the fight, emerging from the command center in ballistic armor like that worn by his men but carrying his staff rather than an automatic weapon. He moved with all the preternatural swiftness of his people, pale and lean and deadly, as we converged on the hunting wolves from two directions.

The security team recognized the friendlies immediately and stopped firing. The wolves, one an odd tan color and the other almost black, seemed confused for a moment and then appeared to recognize their danger. The tan wolf practically screamed a growl and lunged away to meet Al-lin while the black tried to flee.

It is not easy to stand calm in the face of a charging werewolf but Al-lin waited until the tan was within easy range and then used the full powered version of the rune that I had stopped Lon Gifford's shift with all those weeks ago. Ice formed in an instant over the wolf's coat and he went down in a tangle of frozen limbs, his entire body turning to ice from the inside out. Not a particularly pleasant way to die but effective. Al-lin stepped up to the frozen wolf and smashed the yew staff down on the frosted form. The rogue shattered into hundreds of icy shards and Al-lin turned cold, hard eyes on the black wolf as it fled.

My cohort need not have worried. Amber once again demonstrated her superior speed, intercepting the black before he could get through a hole that had somehow appeared in the perimeter fence. The black turned to avoid her snapping jaws and ran directly into me as I made my way forward. I slammed my shoulder into the wolf but he somehow managed to keep his feet in his fear galvanized sprint and turned to slash me across the shoulder with sharp fangs.

The wound hurt and would bleed messily but it really did not slow me down. The effect on Amber though was something that the black wolf had not considered. My mate snarled savagely at the sight of my blood and sprang.

Amber's claws came out as she threw herself onto the back of the black werewolf and he screamed in agony as she clamped down on him, all four sets of claws buried in his back. The two went into a tumbling roll in the snow, red and black alternating and I could see teeth flashing on both sides. I barked sharply at Amber as I approached and she came away from the black as if we had trained together for years.

There was nothing for me to do. Amber had managed to get the other wolf by the back of the neck and had done what she had seen me do a moment before, snapping the black's neck cleanly. There was blood on her fur and I was not sure who it belonged to but, before I could check her out, the second wave arrived.

I had counted the songs of six wolves in the forest but, apparently, one of them had been silent. Looking at the three rogues who now approached, another black, a dark gray and a white with a splash of tan across the shoulders, I saw immediately that Chastel had held his first team in reserve. These three wolves were bigger than the other four and something in the way they moved told me that they had been wolves longer than the first group. I muttered caution at Amber and she shook herself, obviously pulling back on the wild instincts and trying to re-assert more of her strategic mind.

Al-lin might have ordered his people into more easily defended positions but they were not out of the fight. Movement caught my eye from the direction of the little tent city and I saw one of the security triads moving stealthily up along the canvas side of a tent, pausing, and then using a mirror around the corner to ascertain where the enemy was. I cut my eyes toward the troopers and Amber stayed in place with me to see what would happen.

My eyes widened slightly when a series of hand signals passed between the three humans and one of them gestured to a comrade who had concealed himself behind the tent. The rangy security soldier who had come to get Amber and I for a couple of meetings with Al-lin came out from behind the tent with a shoulder carried missile launcher and squatted just behind his comrades.

One of the soldier's in the original triad looked off to the left and I saw that Al-lin had retreated into the tent city as well. Al-lin nodded at his security detail and I saw the lead trooper hold up three fingers and then count down silently by dropping fingers into a fist. On zero, the soldier with the missile launcher stepped calmly from behind the tent, took careful aim and launched.

I don't know the exact speed of a Javelin anti-tank missile but I do know that it clears fifty meters very, very quickly. Judging by the point of impact, the soldier who had used the system had aimed for the center wolf. I dropped to the ground and covered my ears with my paws as best I could in what would have been a comical gesture if it had not been so necessary. Amber realized the danger and followed me a moment later.

CHAPTER THIRTY-TWO

*T*he concussion of the explosion washed over us, followed swiftly by a storm of sound. I noted, with a growl, that some of the blood on Amber's coat was hers. The black wolf had torn a ragged gash in her flank during their tussle. I knew that it would heal spontaneously when she shifted back but that fact did not make me feel better.

Once the dust settled a little, I got to my feet to see if any of the werewolves had managed to escape. I counted two down, the black and the dark gray, but did not see the white. Movement caught my eye out past the perimeter fence and I saw the surviving rogue limping painfully toward the cover of the forest.

Al-lin's people had seen him too and spoke into their radios. From somewhere in the wood, a single shot sounded and the white rogue went down in a boneless heap. I should have known that a group of former special operators would have at least one sniper in a hide somewhere in the area. Sniper rifles come in a variety of calibers but they all have one thing in common—if you hit something with them, that thing basically explodes. I knew that the white rogue was well and truly dead without having to see the corpse melt back to human form. Military snipers are very good at their job and they seldom miss.

I sank slowly to the ground, exhaustion washing over me as the adrenaline washed from my system and Amber came over to nuzzle my neck and whine her concern. Much as I hated to admit it, I was still not fully recovered from the major invocation. I wanted to curl up, right there in the snow, and sleep for a few hours but my mind was whirling. What the hell had Chastel been thinking, throwing a group of relatively inexperienced were-wolves against a camp where he knew there were dangerous humans, a faery lord with magic, a Black Dog, and another werewolf?

I looked around me and realized suddenly that the afternoon was done and the night was falling rapidly.

Almost as if the Beast of Gevaudan had heard my thoughts, I sensed the stirring of dark magic in the air, the hairs of my ruff rising and a low growl escaping me involuntarily. Amber stirred at my side, sniffing the air as though she scented something putrid there, and nudging me to my feet. Slithering cold that had nothing to do with the light wind and snow swept over the camp and I saw Al-lin, still standing off in the tent city, speak into the radio, communicating with his troops. They beat a hasty retreat to some designated area outside of my line of sight as the faery lord stepped into the open, staff in one hand, his own robes draped around him against the cold.

I could not make out the words but a steady droning chant filled the air and a smell like damp earth shoveled from the bottom of a grave came to my sensitive nose. Purple-black fire laced the forest before us, heatless flames licking through the branches, causing Al-lin, who was in touch with every tree spirit in the area, to flinch with pain. The rasping cadence of the chant filled my head, causing it to ache and my eyes to water, as the power gathered, slowly and sullenly beyond the fence.

I knew exactly what was happening but was helpless to stop

it, the weight of my exhaustion and the paralysis of the chart combining to dull my reflexes and make me more than lethargic. I knew that Chastel had learned a way to summon the Black Hag and I could only assume that what we were seeing was the result of a ritual that Chastel was performing somewhere to manifest the Hag. If we did not do something to stop the ancient malevolent faery from manifesting, we were all dead.

* * *

CHASTEL HAD CERTAINLY KNOWN his business but I was not ready to concede the fight. I inhaled, deep into my lungs and then exhaled, expelling the exhaustion from my body. As I had done earlier in meditation, I sent my energy deep into the earth questing for, and finding a tiny ley line to the south of the airstrip. It was not a nexus point but the trickle of power that flowed into me worked well to help me shake off my exhaustion. It was a garden hose rather than a fire hose hooked to a hydrant but it assisted me in clearing my head and preparing my physical form for what was to come.

Al-lin was not ready to concede the fight either. He had been in this camp for a few days and it should have dawned on me that he and the Sigrun would set up some magical as well as mundane defenses. The elf lord walked slowly out onto the airfield, moving slowly and deliberately, making sure that, if Chastel were watching somewhere, he could be seen. Al-lin stopped in a certain spot and scraped his boot over the snow, clearing a small spot down to the ground. He peered at something and then nodded, satisfied that he was in the right place, then inhaling deeply, he vibrated the Word that triggered his defenses.

The faery lord's vibrated Word was not loud but, just for a moment, Chastel's chant seemed to drop into the background. All along the perimeter fence, glass globes, which I had mistaken for old light bulbs, began to glow with an incandescent red light.

Red is a martial color, the color of fire and passion, the hue of those who will not go peacefully. It is the color in which runes are often carved and the Lord of the Runes is, primarily, a god of those who fall in battle. In the myths, and I see no reason to doubt them, it is said that he and one of the Asgardian goddesses have the first pick of the honorably slain.

As I watched, the globes radiated more brilliantly and, as I squinted to look at one of the brilliantly glowing spheres near me, I could see that each glass bulb contained a bind rune carved on a stick of what I presumed was yew. I could not see the entire bind rune through the effulgent, blood red light pouring from the bulbs but I could make out enough of it to know that the basis of the charm was the hunting rune, a rune associated with arrows and carved on a wood traditionally associated with graveyards and thus death.

As the light from the rune bulbs reached its peak and stained the snow red all along the perimeter, I noted that Chastel's chant had shifted to a new and even more urgent rhythm. The voice we all heard had sounded calm and confident at the beginning of the invocation but now sounded strained and harsh. Al-lin smiled wolfishly as I watched and I noted that the headpiece on his staff was glowing with same sanguine light. He and the Sigrun had obviously spent some time putting together this magical perimeter.

I could not see well beyond the perimeter but I sensed that the black flames that had been trying to coalesce in the forest outside the camp had scattered with the onslaught of energy and light from the Al-lin's spell. Still, though, I could hear the chant droning on and I could feel the energy of the Beast's mad rite, though tattered, coming together once more. The defenses would hold for a while but, without a major energy source to power them, eventually, they would fall.

Chastel had obviously planned well for his campaign against us and our team had mostly been reacting to his moves. The

Beast had managed to keep us on the defensive for days now; as my strength returned, anger came with it, hot and stark. I took a moment more to be sure that I had some energy reserves and then quietly broke the connection with the small ley line I had tapped.

I was facing a mortally dire situation now but, unfortunately, I could not perform the classic necromantic death spell on a subject that was out of my line of sight. The Beast knew this and probably thought that he was protected from that aspect of my power. He was wrong.

I stalked out onto the snow, my shining black coat reflecting highlights of blood red in the continued brightness of Al-lin's rune bulbs. I approached but stood away from my friend, wishing I had strength to offer. He was already beginning to sway from the effort of holding the defenses and his knuckles were white where they gripped his staff. I could see that, even with this major Working in progress, the black flames we had seen earlier were beginning to move back into a cogent shape once more. I had a minute, maybe, two before a being from humanity's greatest nightmares manifested.

I did not make a sound to distract Al-lin, just closed my eyes and focused inward, reaching into the fiery core of my being, the part of my Self that makes my eyes glow a sullen red and has given my kind the name Hellhound. The sound that erupted from my muzzle must have sent a frisson through every human in the camp. I would have spared their feelings, had I been able, but the Working that I was forming required that I give full voice to the Call of my kind.

I felt the Call echo out over the woods. Every woodland is a place of death and ghosts; therefore, the forest can be so frightening at night. Prey animals died amongst the trees all the time and the predators that slew them in turn died, victims of larger predators or simply old age. Humans came to the wilds to live out their last days, died in accidents or were taken by their own kind or a rogue from the Other Side. Even the Sasquatch did not live forever; unlike most of faery, the Hairy Ones of the forest lived a long time when they were unmolested but they did move on, deeper into the spirit realms, eventually.

I lifted my muzzle and Called once more, my cry ringing strangely in the snow silent wood. Al-lin had begun a deep counter-chant of his own and was almost unaware of my presence. He was not saving anything back for afterward either.

For a moment, I thought that perhaps Chastel had foxed me here too. The wild land around me remained silent and still and nothing touched my arcane sense. It seemed to me, though, as if the trees themselves held their breath, the only sounds were Chastel's insidious chant and Al-lin's rumbling counter.

It is a paradox to say that the timberland came alive with the dead but that is precisely what happened. The airstrip clearing filled with a sound like wind shrieking through the branches of the birch and oak that surrounded us but not a leaf moved or a dollop of snow fell. Dozens of shades, called from miles around converged on me in a whirling vortex—spirits of fallen pioneers dressed in the garb of another century, soldiers from the Revolution and Civil Wars, clad in their uniforms and carrying arms, victims of tuberculosis, still pale and wasted in death but dressed in their turn of the century finery. These and more came to my Call: hikers and lost children and madmen who had wandered into the wood never to return came. First People who had passed peacefully amongst their beloved mountains and, mixed among them were mortal beings of the Other Side, Sasquatch, and others of the fae who had passed over but chose to answer.

CHAPTER THIRTY-THREE

*A*ltogether, these spirits represented a seething cauldron of energy, one which I did not dare touch since it would pull me in with the dead ones, but one which I could direct. I formed a vision in my mind of Chastel as I had last seen him, standing arrogantly against his vehicle as the demon trap sprang into place. I carved his lean features into my mind, the sneering, crooked smile, and the eyebrows arched with no more than interest as he watched my death descend on me. The spinning wheel of spirits around me shifted slightly, as though picking up a scent and I knew that I had my target. With a booming howl, I released the maelstrom of spirits, sending them to collect the soul of Louis Chastel, if they were able.

A shriek of wild terror sounded from some distance away in the wildwood and the snarling chant ceased. I could not hear distinct words, even in the snow-borne silence, but it seemed to me that I could hear Chastel, crying out in yet another language. The purple-black flames that had been gathering into a recognizable form, dispersed amongst the trees again, still flickering but moving randomly as they lost the matrix of power upon which they were being formed.

All was still for a long moment and I heard Al-lin's chant downshift as the pressure on his magical barrier lessened. I sank to the ground, my head coming to rest in the snow, all of my resources spent. I could not even summon the energy to reach out and touch the vortex I had sent and see if it had claimed its prize. My mind was almost pleasantly blank as I waited to see what would happen next.

I didn't have to wait long. The tornado of shades that I had sent against Chastel exploded, off in the distance, with a sound-less flash of putrid green light, and I felt the snapping of my power as it lashed back at me as the spell imploded. Hundreds of shades were hurled back into the forest, confused and disori-ented, as the magic that had guided them returned to me in a rush, hissing malevolently through me and throwing me violently onto my back. As though he had never stopped, Chastel resumed his chant, even more urgent now that he knew his goal was near.

* * *

I MUST HAVE LOST consciousness for a time. When I recovered myself, I was still lying on my back in the snow. The cold tickled the end of my nose and I sneezed, rolling weakly to my side, and endeavoring, without success, to stand. I was suddenly cognizant of the darkness and silence all around me. The red light of the rune bulbs was out and, as I lifted my head with great effort, I could see Al-lin kneeling in the snow, his sides heaving as though he had just run a long distance. It looked to me as though his staff was the only thing keeping him upright.

A sound like chain link fencing rustling in a high wind caught my attention and I looked up to see the perimeter fence parting as though a steaming brand had been pressed to the surrounding snow. A figure stepped through calmly, looking around and then homing in on me.

I could feel the ancient power seeping over me from meters away as she approached slowly. I remember thinking, in a particularly crazy moment, that this being, this monster of the Other Side, should be bigger. Physically, she was shorter than Amber and wore a flowing black robe that seemed to shimmer and mold itself to her like pipe smoke curling around a static surface.

It was her eyes that made the biggest impression. Like my own, they glowed from within, but unlike mine, the Black Hag's eyes were not red but a violent aquamarine, so bright that they illuminated the depths of the hood, casting sharp cheekbones and slightly pointed ears into sharp relief. There were no pupils to alleviate the foreignness of those eyes and they cast a cold glare as she approached me.

Despondency swept through me in a wave, a depression so thick and black and full of bile that I almost choked on the force of it. Tendrils of that despair crept into every nook and cranny of my mind, convincing me that all was lost, that all that had happened was my fault since I was not good enough, that Amber really felt nothing for me . . .

"That," said a crisp voice in my head, "will be quite enough, Poisoner."

The Black Hag glanced away from me and then sucked in her breath, stepping back a pace. Abruptly, my thoughts came into focus. The Hag had been twisting my thoughts toward self-destruction without me having a clue what was going on. I looked around me blearily, seeking the source of the voice that had pierced the finely woven veil of devastation being cast over me. I let out my breath with a huff when I looked over my shoulder and realized that Amber was standing protectively over me.

I say that Amber was standing over me because it was the beautiful form of my mate that stood there, clad from head to toe in black, but I knew, at a glance, that our desperate gamble had succeeded. I could see my lover looking down at me with concern writ large in her eyes but I could smell the dust, musk, and salt sea tang of the presence of her goddess, Hekate.

* * *

AMBER, who was not really Amber, smiled a cool smile at me and said, "Well met, Black Dog.

I managed to bow my head and chuff a reply and the goddess who had occupied my lover's body laughed, a brittle sound as though She were not yet used to standing in a physical form. "Ah, I had forgotten how good it feels to wear skin. It has been so long since I had an Oracle that I despaired of ever having the sensation again."

I cut my eyes toward the Black Hag standing not three meters away and, again, chuffed, in what I hoped was a polite manner. Amber's eyes, black with her Lady's presence, turned to the ancient faery. "Oh, I do suppose that I have to do something about her, don't I?"

The Hag laughed softly in her throat. "So, this is how the Black Dog and this sorry excuse for a Sidhe lord thought to defeat me? An Oracle channeling a goddess who has not been worshipped in over a thousand years?"

I finally managed to get myself together enough to reply, mind to mind. "Seemed like a good idea at the time." I spared a glance over at Al-lin and saw that he was down. I could not see if he was still breathing. I struggled to control the urge to try to rise and go to him. I suspected that, as with any predatory animal, any sudden moves around the Hag would invoke an aggressive response.

The Hag must have followed the movement of my eyes. She strode over to Al-lin and nudged him with a tiny boot. He stirred, much to my relief, but that relief turned to horror when the Hag drew a sickle-shaped knife from her belt and began to kneel beside him. I recognized the blade; it had been used amongst the Celtic Druids for blood sacrifice long before anyone ever heard of the Romans.

I didn't see Amber move. I did not really know what sort of power the Lady Hekate would be able to bring to bear in this modern age. The issue was still in question but one thing was for certain. The Hag was not going to be using that knife; Amber's form blurred through the air and the knife went sailing over the perimeter fence and into the dark forest.

"Well, Poisoner," Amber drawled in a voice not her own, "it seems that you have lost a step since last we met. Getting slow in your old age?"

The Hag snarled and turned, bearing hands with clawed fingers, and attacked in earnest.

If I had not been barely able to ambulate out of the way, I might have almost enjoyed the fight. Amber/Hekate blocked, parried, and generally shut down her attacker's first flurry of strikes and then opened with an offensive filled with sheer Amber firepower. My lover was an experienced martial artist and, with her goddess riding shotgun, was every bit as swift as the Hag. She moved into a leg sweep that the Hag managed to dodge but reversed the sweep up high, taking the opportunity to crescent kick her opponent neatly in the jaw.

The Hag backed away, swiping wildly with taloned hands, but Amber kept outside the vicious claws, landing damaging blows on her opponent's arms whenever the opportunity presented itself and doing what any good boxer would have done, moving to the outside and punishing the body whenever she could.

Given the amount of abuse her body was taking, the faery changed tactics, tucking her elbows more and moving to keep her clawed defense pointed at her target. The posture looked vaguely like Wing Chun and Amber recognized it immediately and went to her long-range arsenal, pounding the Hag with a dizzying series of kicks and long punches that kept the faery from closing and using the claws inside. One particularly vicious roundhouse seemed to rock the Old One and she staggered.

Only to turn back with a ball of fire in her hand. I started to bark a warning but Amber saw the danger and rolled neatly away from the fireball as it struck the ground and exploded where she had been standing a moment before. "No worshippers indeed. Did I mention," Hekate spat, "that there is now a worldwide group of Hellenic pagans that make offerings to me very regularly and that there are a number of sorcerer's who work under my seal these days."

Amber opened her hand and cast what looked like a net in the Hag's general direction. Fine as spun silk, the interwoven lines of magic glowed faintly with a purple-black light similar to the flames that had heralded the coming of the Black Hag.

Whatever it was, the Hag wanted no part of it. She barked a Word and brilliant light flared in her hand. She threw the light at the net and it dissolved into fine dust. The Hekate who was in Amber raised her eyebrows. "Really, Poisoner, a light spell? Have you fallen so low?"

The counterspell seemed to have winded the ancient faery and she simply glowered and resumed her attack. There were several more passes but it was obvious that the Hag was getting the worst of the punishment. Amber had taken some deep talon slashes along her arms and had been briefly stunned by a balled fist to the temple but, for the most part, she had been dishing out more pain than she had received.

The Black Hag moved to the offensive briefly, sending a withering series of strikes at Amber's head, arms, and shoulders, her hands rolling over to strike as quickly as she could in what Wing Chun practitioners called chain punching. The obvious counter for the chain punching sequence is to get off the line of incoming attack and Amber did this with alacrity, moving and parrying as needed. The faery abruptly broke off her attack as Amber was moving in to counter again and sprang back several meters, throwing her hands up and barking a Word as she sketched a complex interlaced pattern in the air before her. The spell sped toward Amber and I could almost feel the kinetic energy in it from my position a few yards away.

CHAPTER THIRTY-FOUR

*A*mber who was Hekate, turned directly into the incoming magic and thrust her hands forward, snarling a brief spell in the old Greek tongue. The kinetic spell, designed to hurl my lover's body through the fence and smash it against the trees only meters away, broke over her instead, rocking her back hard enough to make her fall to her knees but otherwise leaving her unharmed. Without pause, liquid Greek syllables flowed from my lover's tongue and what looked like a ball of twine appeared in her right hand. With a final exclamation Amber hurled the ball at the Black Hag.

The ancient faery screamed defiance and tried once more to use a spell of light against the incoming twine, which was rapidly unfurling into yet another magical net, this one composed of threads of golden energy that glittered in the dark night. The light spell hit the golden gossamer strands and did absolutely nothing. The net settled over the Hag and contracted dropping her to the ground, thrashing in impotent fury, trying to use her claws to cut the strands away.

Amber who was Hekate walked over to her fallen foe. "Well,

Poisoner, that was amusing, for a time. I think we are done now. It only remains to settle where to put you."

"What are you talking about?" the Hag snarled.

"Well, I do think you have been caged in that cave quite long enough. Don't you agree?"

The Old One looked confused, as though someone had offered her a pickle and given her ice cream instead.

"Oh, do act like one of the Ancient Ones of the Sidhe, Poisoner, not some tongue-tied half-wit."

The Black Hag swallowed hard and composed herself. "Then, yes, I would say that I have spent quite enough time in that cave. Is it any wonder that I wanted to get lose to walk the earth?"

"No wonder at all really and I might have allowed it for a time if you had not been a threat to my Oracle and her mate."

The Hag regarded me with eyes that made me shiver again despite my thick coat. "What do you propose, Lady?" The ancient faery managed to say the honorific without choking on it.

Hekate laughed gaily, "That's the spirit. What would you say if I told you that I could get you a nice spot all your own in Hades?"

The Hag laughed harshly. "You want me to consign myself to one of the hells? I think I would prefer that damned cave."

The goddess who inhabited my lover chuckled, "Oh, heavens no, dear. Nothing so dreary as that, but Hades does have a use for someone of your talents. When you are not working, you would be free to carve out your own little demesne on the Other Side. Interested?"

The Hag eyed Amber and I wondered what it was that she was seeing. "Do I have any other choices?"

Hekate shook her head. "I'm afraid not, dear. I really cannot let you run loose in the Midlands. There's too many of my followers in the way."

The Hag considered for a moment. "Why would you risk opposing the will of the Sidhe courts?"

Hekate laughed again and this time it sounded anything but genuine. "Because, my dear, I am a goddess and sometimes the Old Ones need to be reminded of that."

The Black Hag laughed at that. "Very well, then, Lady, I accept your offer. I speak it twice and agree. I seal it with the third word, accepting your terms and done."

Hekate smiled and took hold of the net as though she intended to haul the ancient faery back to the Underworld by main strength. Instead, she turned and looked at me. "Black Dog, your idea to try to summon me to help in this mess was inspired. By what, I am not sure, but I always have a place at my side for those who are daring and willing to take initiative. If you ever get bored chasing werewolves, talk to my Oracle. I am sure you would make a grand Hound of Hekate."

Before I could do more than gaze at Her in open-mouthed astonishment, She was gone along with her faery package and Amber collapsed to the ground in a dead faint.

I struggled to my feet and made my way over to my lover's fallen body, nudging her with my nose to be certain that her face was not buried in snow. When I was sure that she would be alright for a few moments, I moved over to check on Al-lin. When I huffed on him, he stirred and sat up, looking bleary but getting that calculating look in his eye that said he would be functional soon. I bumped him, too tired to try to speak mind to mind, and moved my eyes toward Amber's prostrate form.

"It worked then?" he queried.

I nodded slowly and he radioed his security team to bring a stretcher and evacuate my mate.

"Chastel?"

I made the dog equivalent of a shrug, too tired to care that I had missed the Beast. If he followed true to form, he had already implemented his escape plan. I was in no condition to do anything more than report just how dangerous the bastard was now. I did not think he would be able to summon the Hag from wherever Hekate took her but he had shown that he was more than capable of using murderous magic to get what he wanted.

Movement caught my attention at that moment and I turned my head lethargically to see what might be moving beyond the perimeter. One of the Sasquatch was standing just past the tree line, gesticulating toward something behind me. I turned my head with more urgency in time to see a gleaming silver ball make a perfect arc and land, not five meters from where I was standing.

Adrenaline poured through my system as I recognized the device. I heard the Sasquatch break into howls all along the tree line and a huge commotion broke out to the west of me. Those facts registered in the back of my mind as I lunged to my feet, grabbed the spherical device in my mouth and whipped my head with all the force I could muster down the airstrip away from anyone who might be approaching now that the fight was supposedly over.

Al-lin's eyes went wide as he recognized the grenade sailing overhead. He jumped toward Amber, pulled his staff to him, and barked the shield rune all in one movement, bringing up a barrier of protection over himself and my fallen mate as she began to stir.

I was outside the protection of that shield and my magic was totally spent. The grenade detonated in a searing flash of light, followed by a shockwave and I passed into darkness, deep and absolute.

* * *

I NEARLY CHOKED to death when I regained consciousness. I opened my eyes to painful light and then someone moved to obscure it, turning it down so that I could see. Even if I had been in my human form, I would have recognized the outline and the scent of the person immediately for she was one of the best known and revered of my kind.

Lael Okiro, one of the senior members of the Black Dog clan council, one of the Old Ones of my people, stood before me. Old habits die hard, I tried to rise, to offer the required respect, but every bone and muscle in my body protested and Okiro placed a restraining hand on my side. "Do not try to move, Black Dog, you have been severely injured. I am here directing the healing."

I managed to look around enough to realize that I was in one of the comfortable, functional rooms in the infirmary at the Wizard's College in Buffalo. I focused my eyes slowly on my senior and managed to communicate quietly, mind to mind. "My mate? And Al-lin of the Greenwood?", I asked, too exhausted to put together full sentences, even for a Dog millennium older than myself.

Okiro's human form was a tall African woman with short, cropped hair and the long neck and graceful limbs of certain tribes in her homeland. Her smile was a bright flash of white against her ebony skin. "It is unorthodox taking a mate who is so new to being a wolf but I have had a chance to talk to her. She is quite able and seems to be adapting well to her new life. She is upright and well although the healers are still working with her energetic system. She woke up temporarily deaf from the explosion but her eardrums have healed. The faery is his usual irascible self, trying to be up and around even though his leg was damaged in the explosion."

"What is important though is that the Beast is no more," she continued.

I almost sat up then but settled for giving her wide eyes, asking for the story silently. She chuffed, as though she were in Dog form and spoke after a moment, "You are either a tactical genius or a complete lunatic, Black Dog. Why on earth did you have armed Sasquatch in the forest?"

I placed my head between my paws and sighed, focusing to

make a reply. "I intended them as scouts only but had them arm to be a distraction if we needed it. Never intended for the fight to come to us—that was Chastel's idea."

Okiro nodded. "Well, given the heavy magic he had been flinging around, Chastel was pretty well depleted when the Sasquatch found him in the forest. They were not able to stop him from using that damned grenade but they made him pay for it and turned his body over to Al-lin in the night. He had been riddled with flint-tipped arrows and the chieftain had broken his spine in several places to be certain that he would never enter their woods again. Sasquatch are normally a gentle people but they can be very territorial if threatened."

I sighed in relief and then my mind moved to its other priority. "Any idea how long I will be down?"

Okiro shrugged. "As long as it takes. You have taken an incredible amount of psychic and physical abuse. I am recommending that we send you off on a rest and rehabilitation trip once you can travel. I have a place in mind and we will deal with the specifics when the time comes."

I nodded and found that my eyes were drooping. Okiro dropped a friendly hand onto my coat. "I know you are weary but your mate has been militating to see you for days. We only kept her out by telling her it would be bad for you to be disturbed. Shall I get her for you?" I summoned the strength to huff affirmatively.

Amber appeared in the doorway a moment later and her eyes filled with tears when I returned her gaze. She looked wan and her eyes had dark circles under them but I have never seen a more welcome sight.

She came slowly across the room and sat carefully on the side of the bed, placing a hand on my flank. I tried to move closer to her but the effort was too much for me. She lay down slowly behind me and pushed her face into the ruff of fur around my neck. I did not try to say anything and she did not speak. Before I was even aware of it, I had fallen back asleep.

EPILOGUE

Once the immediate danger to my life was over, the Council had arranged for me to spend time at a beach resort owned by Other Side interests in Costa Rica. I spent my days doing slow Bagua in the morning, lounging on the beach in the afternoons and getting increasingly longer runs in, with my mate by my side, in the dense jungles just outside the compound.

My overblown sense of duty began to kick in after a couple of weeks of this and I had to endure the wrath of my mate when I suggested that it might be time for me to get back to work. "Zach, what are you thinking? Do you really understand how close we came to losing you? Three weeks ago, Al-lin pulled your smoking body onto a helicopter and trundled me into the chopper as well, still half-conscious, after doing my first major Work."

I started to speak but she cut me off with a look. "On that fifth day, when Ms. Okiro came out to get me and told me I could finally see you, it was the first time I had slept for more than a couple of hours. Know why?"

I shook my head. I knew there was more for her to say. "Because I put my nose on you and felt the warmth of you through your fur and knew, in some way that I do not understand, that you were going to be okay, that you would come out of this whole. All I had to do was take care of you and make sure that you healed thoroughly."

"So, Mr. hard-headed Black Dog, if you pick up that phone and try to call Lael Okiro and tell her that you are ready for work, she is going to hang up and call me." Amber held up her cell phone. "And I am not letting you go back until I am certain that you are 100% or better."

There was not much I could say to that. Instead, I stood up and gestured for her to come walk with me. Once we were down the beach a way, the warm wind blowing off the Atlantic bringing the smell of brine to our noses, I took her hand and squeezed. It took me a moment to get words out past the lump in my throat. "I am sorry. I would never have put you in that situation if I could have avoided it."

My mate nodded. "I know and I know that part of why I love you is your sense of duty and your honor. I know that this is not the last time you will be in danger. And it probably will not be the last time you are injured. I have to live with that but, if I am going to live with it, for the many years we have before us, you will have to give a little on your side and allow me to take care of you and make sure you are back together before I allow you to be thrown back into the fray."

I looked into her green eyes, saw the raw emotion there and pulled her to me. Amber dropped her head onto my shoulder and sighed, her arms holding me firmly for the first time since I had been injured. I smiled against her warm hair and spoke when I felt I could trust my voice, "I accept your terms with one condition."

My mate looked up at me sharply, "No conditions, buster. I will sic the Old One on you in a heartbeat."

I held up my hands in mock surrender. "My only condition is this, that the same will apply if something happens to you. As you have discovered, you cannot be," I hesitated for just a moment, "mated to a Black Dog and not get pulled into my life sometimes. You need to know and understand that if our situations were reversed, I would be just as cautious with you."

Amber hugged me fiercely, her hot cheek pressed against my bare chest. "I can live with that," she said after a moment.

I laughed and stroked her hair, kissing her firmly before we continued our stroll down the beach, relishing the companionable silence between us.

ABOUT THE AUTHOR

W T Watson is a coffee addict with an abiding love of monsters, magic, Forteana and the paranormal that infuses his fictional works. When he is not writing or reading about monsters, he can be found outdoors allowing his dogs to take him for a walk around his neighbourhood in Kitchener, Ontario. He lives with his spouse, Stacey, in a townhome that would be jammed with books if it weren't for e-readers.